# THE EYES OF SPIES

## IVORY TOWER SPIES  BOOK TWO

### EMILY KAZMIERSKI

Also by Emily Kazmierski

Ivory Tower Spies Series

*For Your Ears Only*
*The Walk-in Agent*
*The Eyes of Spies*

Other Works

*Malignant*
*Life Among the Ashes*
*All-American Liars*

To our law enforcement officers, first responders, and military personnel around the world, thank you for fighting to keep us safe, especially when we don't understand the cost.

# Prologue

My watch pings, but I ignore it. I already have a ton of missed messages from Royal, Clarity, Lotus, and even Julep, asking where I am. I half expect Royal's voice to start yelling in my ear, but then I remember I'm not wearing my earbud. It's in my bag in the trunk of the rental car. I've only been AWOL from my teammates for three days, but Royal has already tracked me through my watch and knows exactly where I am—Alabama. The real question is why he hasn't come after me yet. Maybe he thinks if he gives me enough rope I'll guilt myself into coming back without him having to come down on me. And you know what? He's probably right. I've never just up and left my team, my family, before, but I had to. Even if I can't say goodbye to Vale's parents, I had to come see where they lay him in the ground to rest. At least I'll be able to picture the site in my mind in the future, like I do with my mom's resting place.

I take a deep breath and focus on the gathering to my right, in the middle of the graveyard. Sun streams down over everything, making the funeral-black of the cluster of mourners across the way seem harsh and loud despite the fact that I can't hear more than a stray sob now and then under the minister's soft, soothing voice. It's like someone has taken a picture and ratcheted up the contrast and black point way too high.

One of the mourners turns away from the service, toward me, and coughs into her hand. I duck down lower in my car to avoid being seen. No one will recognize me in my oversized, dark sunglasses, brunette wig, and navy shift dress, but I don't want to answer any questions as to why I'm hiding in a vehicle when a burial service is being held a hundred feet away.

*Cameron Walker Lewis.*

Vale's real name.

He had told me he was from Alabama, and that his parents were former analysts for the CIA, but he'd never told me his real name. Well, I'd never asked. Vale would have told me if I had—a hushed secret in a stolen moment away from the rest of our team.

My insides heat at the memory of his arms around me, the way he smiled at me when we were alone, his confidence in my feelings for him, up until our last couple weeks, when he'd been frustrated with me for refusing to tell Royal about our relationship. Maybe if I hadn't kept putting him off, he wouldn't have pushed for a spot in the field. I can't help but wonder if he was trying to prove to Royal, to me, that he was good enough. Maybe if I had agreed to fess up to my dad, Vale—no, Cameron—would still be alive, sitting at his laptop, running our communications when we're in the field. The voice behind the curtain, as it were.

Despite all the blinking I can muster, my eyes water. When I'm finally able to see through them again, the service is drawing to a close. I have to get out of here before someone sees me and grows suspicious, or worse, strikes up a conversation.

I start the car and back out down the narrow concrete

pathway, but a flash of movement stops me. A figure, a person I never thought I'd see, flits in my peripheral vision. I spin my head to get a better look, but she's no longer there. The graveyard is empty, and the face burned into my view must have been a figment of my imagination.

There's no possible way my mother was here in this graveyard, watching me watch my boyfriend be buried. I shake it off and point the car toward the airport. It's time to get back to DC and whatever punishment Royal has waiting for me when I return to the Ivory Tower.

# Chapter 1

**Six months later**

The wind whips around the skyscraper and slams into my body. I steady my hands as I replace the panel of glass I'd cut through four minutes before. It almost falls through into to the darkened office on the other side, but I catch it just in time. I rush through melding the glass back together with my handheld laser welder since the staff at Cobalt Services, from what I've heard, are not to be messed with. Tightening my grip on the rope that suspends me, I begin pulling myself upward, but movement inside the building catches my eye. The Cobalt security personnel have arrived.

The men, who are wearing black suits with white shirts and black ties, run into the office I have just vacated, their guns drawn and eyes darting around. Despite the generic look of their uniforms, I'm hoping they don't spot me.

But everything doesn't always go my way.

One of them locks his eyes on me and murmurs to the

others without taking his eyes off me.

As one unit, the men move toward the window with guns aimed right at my head.

I don't hesitate. In one swipe, I pull my tactical knife out of my utility belt and sever the rope above my head.

My body is plummeting toward the ground.

"You cut the rope!" Lotus yells through my earbud, his voice incredulous. "Do you need help? Oh geez, I see you. I'm coming down." The sound of him ziplining to the roof of the next building and scrambling down the fire escape reaches my ears, but I don't respond.

I curl my feet up toward my butt and loosen my arms so they fly up on either side of my face. I can't say that I've done much urban skydiving, so I'm focused on the asphalt below me, waiting as long as possible before deploying my chute.

Three

Two

One

The powerful jolt of my parachute opening yanks on my pelvis. It's at once painful and reassuring. Grasping the steering cords on my chute with steady hands, I steer away from the towering glass edifice I've just left. I have to get as far away as I can before their security personnel reach ground level.

I'm low enough now that if I'm within range when they spill out onto the street, they'll shoot at me. And most likely they won't miss.

I glide around the corner, losing altitude the entire way. "Meet me in the alley," I say, knowing my earbud will pick it up.

"Will do," Lotus says.

My heart is still pounding. That was close. A grin settles on my face. I've done it. The thumb drive is in my utility belt.

I bend my knees and brace for impact with the concrete, but my feet slam into the ground and my legs crumble, casting me face-first onto the cement. A frustrated groan escapes me as the crisp, white canopy of the parachute billows down around me. After jumping to my feet, I cut the cords. There isn't time to fold the chute properly, so I ball it up and shove it into a trashcan on the sidewalk. Pumping my legs, I bolt around the corner of the building into the dark alley.

Behind me, footsteps pound the pavement. Cobalt's security force is catching up.

Crap.

My eyes dart over the long, narrow space. The only hiding place is a large, dingy blue dumpster. Of course. I hurl myself over the side and into the dank black of the giant metal box. The squishy, smelly scent of rotting food folds over me. I move my hips back and forth, slithering down into the garbage. Gooey liquid seeps down my neck into my bodysuit. I breathe through my mouth to avoid the rank smell. Why is it that whenever I need shelter in a situation like this, there's never an industrial sized recycling bin around? Shredded paper would be infinitely preferable to the putrid goop I've found myself in in the past.

"Where are you?" Lotus's voice hums in my ear.

I don't respond as I reach down to unclip my handgun from its holster at my waist. If Lotus is close by he can hear what I'm hearing, and he'll understand.

Heavy boots clump around the corner and halt mere feet from my hiding place.

I breathe silently, slowly, hoping they won't look in the dumpster, but of course they do.

The dumpster eases back toward the wall as a large someone leans over it to peer inside, the metal groaning under the force.

My eyes are wide open, despite the burning starting due to the muck I'm in. I'm staring at the garbage bag above my face, hoping they don't start digging through the trash. It would only take one swipe of the hand for them to spot me, and then I'd be done. I'd be another in the long line of people who have simply disappeared. It takes all of my training to keep calm in this moment, a breath away from oblivion. My hands are wrapped tightly around my weapon, but I'm praying I don't have to pull the trigger. An image of bloody hands flashes in my mind's eye.

Come on, Loveday. Focus. I push the image away.

The metal box squeaks as the weight eases off the dumpster and the footsteps move away down the alley.

I take a deep breath in through my nose, but regret it immediately when the stench of eggshells hits my throat.

Stifling the urge to gag, I whisper. "I'll meet you behind the bank in one minute."

"I'm already here," comes Lotus's response. "I had to duck out of the alley to avoid the suits. Where are you?"

I ignore it. He'll be able to smell where I was soon enough.

Easing myself into a crouching position, I straighten my legs and peek over the edge of the dumpster. The Cobalt security force is nowhere in sight. I take a deep breath and hoist myself out of the bin, pushing my legs to their limit. I bolt out of the alley and around the corner to the bank building. It's only fifty yards away.

A shot rings out behind me.

I don't dare look over my shoulder as I round the corner.

Lotus is there on his Suzuki, waiting for me.

Taking a running leap, I jump on the back of the motorcycle and snake my arms around Lotus's waist. "Go!"

He guns it.

Several more gunshots reach my ears, but no pain bites into my body.

"That was close," Lotus yells as he maneuvers the bike down the street.

My heart is pounding in my chest, but I know what'll ease the tension. I lean closer to Lotus, digging my pointy chin into the space between his shoulder blades and rubbing in sloppy circles. He's super ticklish here, which I found out by accident when I poked him in the back once.

Lotus screeches and arches forward away from me without letting go of the handlebars. "Stop that!" he pleads between peals of laughter. "Not while I'm driving!" As if to prove his point, the Suzuki jerks to the right, toward the curb.

"Point taken," I yell in his ear. Without looking back, I retrieve the helmet from the storage box over the back wheel and pull it on over my mousy brown wig, a smile settling over my face.

We've done it. Once we get home, Royal, with Haru's help, will be able to dig into Cobalt's recent activities to see if they've been breaking the law like the CIA suspects.

It's barely 05:00, but the streets are already teaming with commuters. Even so, no one notices us as Lotus weaves expertly between vehicles on the road. People are not nearly as observant as they think they are. They miss pretty much everything.

# Chapter 2

Lotus drops me at the hotel's staff entrance and pulls his motorcycle around the corner toward the parking garage exit.

The hall is warmly lit when I step inside. I pass the employee locker rooms, laundry, and supply closets and step into the kitchen. There are only a couple of staffers present, beginning work on breakfast for the buffet. One is muttering to herself as she gathers dry ingredients from the pantry. The other is leaning against the counter nursing a large mug of coffee. Neither one looks particularly alert. My mouth tilts upward. It's a risk I'll take. Neither of them notices me as I duck below the counter and approach the pantry. The woman who was digging around inside seems satisfied with the load of cartons in her arms, because she shuffles around the counter to the other side, near the industrial stove. I peer over the countertop, but coffee girl hasn't seen me either. Snaking one arm above the counter, I swipe a couple kiwis from the bowl and eat them, skin and all. They tickle on the way down, which is why I love them so much. No other fruit does that.

I pivot where I'm squatting near the floor and stare at the

fridge thermostat for a minute, itching to try the new entrance Royal has installed to our bunker. The door from the dining room swings open and three more kitchen staffers enter the room. I frown silently. I've missed my chance. Keeping low, I scuttle back through the kitchen and out into the staff tunnel. But instead of moving back toward the parking garage, I continue down the hall toward the lobby. The hotel is a giant cube, with rooms on all four sides facing inward toward the atrium. I crane my neck to look up at the ceiling, a glittering space of glass through which the stars twinkle and blink, shining brightly before fading as dawn breaks.

Since it's so early, the atrium is mostly empty.

There's one hotel patron at the ATM, standing still so the facial recognition software can connect his visage to his account.

I move carefully toward the pond and waterfall that stands in the center of the open space, glowing vivid blue from the lights mounted at the bottom of the pond. One by one, I cross the stepping stones and duck behind the waterfall. A lever, labeled "Waterfall Maintenance," sits against the slimy wall, its rubber coating peeling in places. I pull it downward, and a door in the back wall slides open. I step down into the doorway and push a silver button on the wall. The door grinds closed behind me.

When they built this place, Darnay told everyone it was a conference facility, and the brainless baboons bought it. A smirk rises to my lips. Charles Darnay isn't much more than a baboon himself. My mind never can quite wrap around the idea that he was a spy in the glory days when my dad was active. Well, more active. And especially not after the London fiasco.

The steps down to the Ivory Tower, our home base, are lit by tube lights that flank the stairs. At the bottom, a thick metal door blocks my way. I step to my right and stand with my nose a hair's breadth away from the facial scanner, which is a black, 4" square panel mounted on the wall. It beeps three times, letting me know it's scanned and recognized my features, and the metal door slides into the wall, opening the path forward.

Lotus's helmet hangs on a peg on the wall, next to an assortment of jackets, scarves, and accoutrements, but he's not in the den. Wall sconces light the room dimly, favoring the two mismatched sofas and handful of plush chairs that sit in what amounts to a circle.

I pull my trench coat off one of the hooks and put it on, buttoning it securely.

Haru bounces toward me, clapping her hands together in rapid motion. "Did you get it? Did you? Did you?" Her entire body hums with kinetic energy, and she swipes at the inside of her right elbow with her left hand. It's an unconscious fidget of hers.

"Yeah." I pull the thumb drive out of my belt and hand it over.

"Yes!" She pumps her fist and shoots away from me toward the control room.

I use my mug to unlock another facial recognition panel and step into the armory. It's a long, narrow room lined with gun safes. We each have one. Well, Haru doesn't. She's only been down in the Tower with us a month and her weaponry skills aren't great, not that she needs them. Royal won't ever put her in the field. But already her computer and coding skills have come in handy.

The safes are lit by cold, white lights that shine upward from the floor. I walk over to my safe and place my right hand flat on the screen set into the middle of the door panel. A small red light in the upper right corner of the screen blinks several times before turning green. I spin the five-pronged handle and pull open the heavy, 6" thick steel door.

A corner of my lip curls up at the sight of my arsenal. I *may* have a few firearms. I stow my Glock and ammo in their proper places, along with my tactical knife. My karambit knives stay on my belt at all times. I close the safe before putting my rappelling gear in the inner room of the armory. It's a small room made of floor-to-ceiling wire mesh cages with everything from binoculars and other surveillance devices to ropes, parachutes, etcetera. I take a deep breath as my eyes rove over the shelves filled with trimmings of my trade. The order of the armory is soothing. I could defend myself against pretty much anyone using the tools we keep here.

I pull the bobby pins out of my hair, and whip off the wig. My scalp is itchy under the cap. My bleached, white-blonde hair is slicked back. The roots are dark. Thankfully, Clarity loves extending her cosmetic experimentation to me, and anyone else who will sit still long enough. One time, Clarity accidentally on purpose dyed my hair bright pink with a natural, beet juice dye she wanted to test.

My scalp tingles as I dig my fingers into my hair, mussing my faux hawk so it flops down to the left. The short hair on the sides of my head is pressed flat, but once I'm done rubbing my skin, it's probably sticking out in all directions.

Hoping to avoid Royal, I duck past the control room and into the dormitory. Clarity has added photos of Rihanna to the collage surrounding our door in the few hours I've been gone.

She's there when I shut the door behind me, her long, thick body curled over her vintage, mirrored vanity, makeup strewn across its surface. She turns to me with a broad smile.

I bust up laughing.

Two of her teeth are blacked out and she's sporting a

unibrow.

"Who are you today?"

She shrugs. "Just experimenting."

Once I'm clean and changed, I return to my room.

Clarity is still at her desk, inches away from her mirror, putting finishing touches on her eyebrows.

I slide open the bottom right drawer of my desk and kiss a finger before pressing it to my mother's photograph, then to Vale's. The new, shiny black frame doesn't jibe with the older, scratched frame around my mother, but I won't change it. An old loss and a new one, side by side. I run a finger over the bindings of my mom's old, cloth bound books. The gold lettering is fading, and the pages are bent and yellowed, but they're my most prized possessions: the only tangible remnants of my mother. I pick up a small, blue volume, Lucy Maud Montgomery's *Anne of Green Gables*, and tiptoe back across the room to sit at Clarity's feet. She pats my hair absently, says, "We'll bleach this later," and returns her focus to the mirror.

Lotus pops his head in the door. "Royal's called a briefing."

A glance at my watch shows no new notifications. "Why not send a message?"

Lotus shrugs. "I was heading this way anyway."

A sigh escapes as I close my book. I cross the minefield that is our room and set the book back in its drawer where it will be safe.

Clarity stands, stretching her arms and back and making a low groan as she does so. "I've been at that desk for way too long," she says, moving to the door.

"Are you going to take out those black teeth?" I cock my head at her.

"And miss the look on Haru's face? No way." She prances

19

out of the room with what I know is a Cheshire cat smile spread across her lips. She loves to creep out Haru with her experiments.

# Chapter 3

I pop the earbud back in my ear and follow Clarity down the hall to the control room.

Royal is already there, waiting next to the large screen that covers the entire wall at the far end of the room. It's covered in data that scrolls up the screen too quickly for me to read.

Haru is sitting at one of the two desks directly in front of the screen, typing away on her laptop.

I sidle up to her, glancing at Royal as I move. "Get what we need?"

"Eep!" She jumps and turns to me. "You scared me."

"Sorry."

She gives me a wide, perky smile before returning her attention to her computer screen. "It's okay. And I'm working on it."

Beside her, Lotus is practicing on the flight simulator on his laptop. He lands the computer-generated plane easily. "See?! Number two hundred."

"Simulations," I say, crossing my arms.

"So?" he shoots at me, then simmers down. "I can do it in

real life too, if he'd let me." He shoots a look at Royal, his lower lip sticking out. Lotus has had his pilot license for a couple months, but Royal still won't let us go up for a ride without him chaperoning, not since the incident with the squirrel on the runway.

I can't hide the smirk. "He'll come around." I look over my shoulder at Royal. "Maybe."

I move to sit near my sister, who has claimed her usual spot on the couch at the side of the room. She kneads the pillows like a cat before nestling in. Her eyes flick up to my hair as I spin and sit on the carpet at her feet, my back pressed against the front of the couch.

I turn my eyes to Royal. He stands with arms folded, his clear blue eyes not missing anything.

Once we are all seated, Royal speaks. "First, well done Lotus and Loveday for retrieving the data we needed." He looks at me, his eyes boring right through me.

My hackles rise.

He is not happy.

"Haru has begun digging around in the data we stole from Cobalt Services, and we were right. They've been selling decommissioned weapons to both sides of the conflict in the Middle East. Good job, Loveday, Lotus." He pauses, his mouth a thin line as he looks at me. Then he clasps his hands and continues. "But the CIA wants us to focus on a different, more emergent problem. I just heard from my contact that XCom's facial recognition software has been stolen."

"That's not good," I say, mouth agape.

"No it isn't," Royal says. "CIA analysts believe the thief— a black market information vendor known as The Chin—is planning to sell the software at a secret auction, like he's done with sensitive information in the past."

"The Chin? Did Leno get a new gig?" Lotus quips.

Haru giggles, only stopping when Royal levies his weighty stare at her.

"Sorry." She touches her computer screen and a photo pops up on the large screen at the front of the room.

I can see why the guy is called The Chin. He's bald, with normal sized features, except for his large, protruding chin. His clothes are well-worn but not to the point of being shabby, and he's got small, round sunglasses over his small eyes.

"You can imagine the implications of the sale of any gathered information." Royal says to regain our attention. He runs a finger across the skin under the band of his watch. "We'll be sending a team to Russia to intercept The Chin before he can find buyers for all of the data he's collected. The team roster will be finalized in two days, after some specific training exercises." He claps once. "Moving on." He gestures toward the door that leads from the control room into his office, and a new guy walks in. He's probably around twenty years old, and dude is tall. I mean, I'm only 5'2", but wow. He would have made even Vale look like a shorty. The way he stands, feet apart, hands behind his back, indicates he's had military training.

I narrow my eyes. We don't need any new players.

"This is Starling," Royal says, patting the new guy on the shoulder. "He's joining our team. Julep's got him into shape for us. I'm sure all of you will make him feel welcome here." His eyes rest on me, daring me to say something.

I clench my jaw, not rising to the challenge. Ever since we lost Vale he has been testing me, waiting to see if I'll break. I won't.

# Chapter 4

"This is ace," Starling says, a wide grin on his face. He's got a London accent. "I'm excited to meet everyone. I've been working toward this for a long time."

I fight the urge to raise an eyebrow. He's been here all of two minutes and his eager attitude is already making me want to hurl.

Lotus stands from his desk and walks over to Starling, sizing him up before grinning.

I roll my eyes.

"So… Starling?" He holds up a hand for a high-five, and Starling responds in kind.

"That's right. They're brilliant birds, starlings."

"Cool," Lotus says. He introduces himself. "So, what're your skills?"

The new guy gives a confident grin. "Hand to hand combat, weaponry, parachuting, tactics in the field, that sort of thing."

My mouth drops open slightly. He's the male version of me. Those are my skills.

"I'm our resident transportation expert," Lotus says.

Starling nods, hitching a thumb in his belt. "Sweet. So you've got the cool rides, eh?"

"That's right," Lotus says, his chest puffing up. And he's right. After the London job, Darnay let Lotus keep the Suzuki and one of the BMW 7 Saloons. Darnay offered them to Clarity and me as well, but we declined. Royal lets us use his boring old Civic when we need a vehicle, and we've found that we blend much better in an old beater than we would in cars with that kind of swank.

I glance around for something to chuck at the back of Lotus's oversized, brown head.

Clarity puts a hand on my shoulder to still me.

I take a deep breath. Their chatter gives me time to size up the newcomer. Starling must be around six foot five. He has an angled jaw, narrow eyes under straight, black eyebrows, full lips, and warm, fawn brown skin. I hate him.

Haru is chattering away at him about surveillance and monitoring us while we're in the field.

Clarity stands up, her calf brushing against my shoulder as she moves toward them.

"Loveday," Royal says. It's the flat way he says it that catches my attention. I'm in trouble. He points in the direction of his office and I follow him into the small room, closing the door behind me.

His desk, made of an old airplane wing, sits in the center of the space. A framed photograph, and Royal's tablet and earbud are all that sit on the surface of the battered, scuffed metal.

He sits in his black desk chair, steepling his fingers.

I square my body over my feet and hold my head high.

"You ignored communication again."

"I couldn't let the security clones at Cobalt hear me."

"That is no excuse. You had your watch."

"What was I supposed to do? Type a message with my hand while lying underneath a pile of rotting, disgusting food?"

He grits his teeth. "Don't let it happen again. I'm this close to…" He trails off, holding his thumb and pointer finger a mere hair's breadth away from each other.

"What are you going to do? This is *my* team."

"Watch it," he says. "You're on thin ice."

I bite the inside of my lip to avoid glaring at him. It's obvious he's mad at me. He's been short with me for six months, ever since I made an unauthorized trip down to Alabama to watch a family I had never met lower Vale's body into the ground in a shiny mahogany casket.

But Royal couldn't afford to bench me. I lead this team when we're in the field, so any threats to the contrary he might have made would have been hollow.

Then it occurs to me. He doesn't need me with Starling here. But maybe that's the point. Kick me off the team now that he's found Starling. The thought rankles in me, screwing up my insides into a twisted, molten lava knot.

"I don't need this," I say. I stalk out to the living room, plop down sideways in one of the chairs with my back propped against one arm and my legs slung over the other, and open the news on my watch. The top video is a snippet of Darnay making a fool of himself, yet again. He went and fell into the fountain at one of his hotels. He is such an imbecile. I can't believe he was once a spy with my dad. He seems to be the exact opposite of everything a spy should be. He's obvious and loud, and in all of the publicity footage I've seen, he moves like an orangutan, all elbows, knees, and feet.

My mind is reeling. Everyone on the team knows that I

have been off since Vale died, less communicative. They've been waiting for me to get back on my game, but I haven't been able to do it. Maybe I can't anymore. And now with Starling here, I may not get another chance.

# Chapter 5

Speaking of, the newbie slips into the den, moving gracefully despite his tall, lanky figure.

"I didn't get a chance to introduce myself to you." He stands beside my chair, looking down at me.

I silence my watch and stand. "No need." I move past him toward the dormitory.

"Wait, please."

The earnestness in his voice makes me pause. It's not his fault I've been off my game, after all. I turn slowly toward him and look up into his face. The way he's looking at me, pleading with his eyes, makes my stomach roll. I shove my irritation down and tilt my head. "Yes?"

Starling gives an easy smile. "I've been looking forward to meeting you. Julep has told me quite a lot about you. It's all very impressive."

Irritated again. He's heard so much about me, but I haven't heard a peep about him until five minutes ago. "Whatever. It's the job."

"No seriously, you're the best teenaged espionage agent

I've ever heard of. You're like a legend."

All of this flattery is getting you nowhere, newbie. "What do you want?"

His eyes widen. Clearly, he's surprised by my abrupt behavior.

I wait.

His face relaxes, and he tries again. "I was sorry to hear about Vale. I know he was your partner—"

"Never mention Vale to me again." I spin on my heel and leave the room. Once I'm in the hallway to the dormitory, I lean back on the wall, listening to make sure he isn't following me. The last thing I want from him is pity over losing Vale. He has no idea what it's like.

There isn't any movement from the living room, which means that Starling is probably standing there with an expression of confusion on his face. He was probably expecting a welcome party. Well, he's not getting one.

A tiny, round speaker on the ceiling beeps once, bringing me to attention. Someone is coming in the front entrance. I open the surveillance feed on my watch.

It's Charles Darnay. What is that clown doing here?

I move out of the dormitory toward the control room, but Darnay beats me there. He's giving Royal a bear hug when I walk in.

"I'm happy to be here. My trip around Europe was rather tiring." He drags a hand down his face, scratching his skin through his scruffy, closely cropped, salt and pepper beard. I've heard him give interviews before, but still his London accent surprises me. It gives his voice a pleasant, proper sound.

My dad laughs heartily as he glances down at Darnay's soft midsection. "It looks like you've been eating too many pastries, my friend."

Starling slides into the room, stopping just behind me, his body tensing at the sight of both men. He swallows before putting on a wide-eyed smile. He's starstruck. Oh brother.

Darnay and Royal look up at us. It's as if they didn't notice until this moment that we are in the room with them.

"So, this is your new recruit?" Darnay smiles and moves toward us, holding out a hand.

Starling takes it. "Hi. You can call me, um…"

"Starling," Royal supplies. "He joined us this morning. I'm looking forward to starting team exercises in just a few hours. You'll stay and observe, I hope?"

Darnay nods. "Wouldn't miss it."

Royal turns to me. "Loveday, why don't you show Starling to the dormitory? I put him in the room across from mine."

A stab of pain shoots through me. That was Vale's room. I spent a lot of time there. My eyes flick up to Royal's face, and the serious look in his eyes keeps me from voicing the argument on the tip of my tongue. "Fine. Come on." I walk down the hall to the dormitory, wishing I had heavy boots to stomp as I went. But heavy boots really aren't my style. They're too loud. Everyone would hear me coming. Instead I'm wearing my usual nondescript black athletic shoes with grips on the bottom.

I stop just inside the dormitory hallway and gesture to the closed, white door. "Here you go." I swing the door open but hesitate in the doorway. This room looks eerie without Vale's chocolate-brown bedding and his bookshelf stacked with cookbooks.

"Go on in," I say, stepping back to let Starling pass.

Starling smiles at me as he moves purposefully past me, into the dorm room. "Thanks."

Moving down the hall, my eyes skirt over the colorful

photos around the door to the room I share with my sister. I grit my teeth as I enter, closing the door behind me.

Clarity's at her desk again, removing the black fronts from her teeth.

I stand against the closed door, my hands resting on my hips. "He's trying to replace me."

# Chapter 6

Clarity sits back from her mirror and turns to face me. "No, Sis, he's not." She stands and puts an arm around me, squeezing my arm lightly. "Come on." She pushes me toward my bed.

With my back to the bed frame, I take off my utility belt.

Clarity takes it from me and sets it on my desk with a light thunk. "Get some sleep," she says with a pat on my cheek.

I start to argue, but the fatigue from being up all night is starting to hit me. After kicking off my shoes, I climb the ladder to my lofted bed. A contented sigh escapes as I curl up under the navy blue down comforter. "Wake me for lunch." I'm out before Clarity can respond.

My eyes pop open at the click of the door. I sit bolt upright, my eyes scanning the room. Clarity isn't here. She must have just left.

I throw off my comforter and slide off the edge of the bed, falling the five feet to the ground. My watch reads 05:32 as I fasten it to my left wrist. I glance down at my trench coat; it's wrinkled. I should have taken it off before my nap. Oh well.

I stride down the hall toward the den. It serves as the center of our existence: all the rooms in the Ivory Tower shoot off it like spokes on a bicycle wheel. As I approach the kitchen, I smell yakisoba. A smile plays on my lips. It's Haru's turn to cook dinner, and that means Japanese food.

I step down into the kitchen, surrounded by concrete walls. The work surface is a concrete island that runs the length of the space, and it holds both the gas stove and a deep, stainless steel sink. Haru stands at the stove, working over two different woks. The food is sizzling in the pans. It smells delicious.

Across from the concrete mass that is the kitchen, a long trestle table sits surrounded by an assortment of metal chairs. Large, black pendant lights hang low over the table's surface.

Lotus and Starling sit on one side of the table, playing with a couple of Lotus's handheld games.

Clarity sits in her usual spot at the head of the table, legs curled under her, reading a book. It's *The Bluest Eye* by Toni Morrison today.

"It smells good." I grin at Haru as I enter the room.

"Thanks! It's yakisoba noodles. I've got options for vegetarians and carnivores alike." She beams.

"Great." I approach the table and sling my trench coat over the chair next to Clarity.

Lotus gives me a grunt without looking up from his video game.

Starling throws his game down on the table and stands up, his chair clattering to the floor. "Uh, do I salute?" he asks. "How does this work?"

Lotus bursts out laughing. "We're not in the military. You can chill."

Starling's eyes don't leave my face, which I fight to keep blank, expressionless.

"I'd prefer a curtsey," I deadpan. I cock an eyebrow at him.

His eyebrows rise; he's wondering if I'm serious.

I don't give him any indication that I'm kidding. Instead, I stare him down, challenging him to react.

He doesn't move for a beat, but then he does what I assume is his best curtsey, a small smile on his face.

Lotus guffaws and Haru chitters from her place at the stove.

"At ease." I slide into the chair next to Clarity, who shoots a reproachful look at me before going back to her book.

Starling rights his chair and sits down. "I meant what I said earlier," he says sincerely, gazing at me. "I've heard a lot about you. Julep filled me in during training. I'd really like to hear your take on your trip to South Korea. How did you sweet-talk your way into the demilitarized zone?"

The image of a selfie flashes into my brain. It's me, sandwiched between two South Korean military personnel, and wearing a hot orange tube top and the most voluminous, ditzy-looking blonde wig Clarity owns. It was an epic day.

"It's classified."

"Oh. Sorry." Starling blinks but doesn't look away.

"She's kidding," Lotus says with an elbow to Starling's arm. "They sent her out there to get a read on the situation after that kid defected from North Korea. They figured she'd be less conspicuous than Royal. Nobody suspects a tiny female dressed in a tube top."

"Ain't that the truth," Julep chimes in.

We all whip around as she walks into the kitchen, her long box braids swinging from side to side at her back. She's wearing a bright pink blouse, a charcoal gray pencil skirt, and black booties. And she is sizzling.

"Damn," Lotus says, eyes wide.

"Drink it in," Julep says, all pomp and sass. "It's all you're gonna get." But her smile creeps up to her eyes.

I smile. "Welcome back."

"Thanks." She ruffles my hair. "How's it hanging?"

"To the left."

She laughs, brassy and loud.

"Sausage fest, remember?"

"Not anymore," she says. "We've got them outnumbered now." She turns to Clarity. "*The Bluest Eye*. That's one of my favorites."

Clarity nods. "It's riveting."

"True." Then to Starling. "How's your first day going? Get in good with the boss?"

Starling's eyes flick to me and back to her.

Julep laughs. "I was talking about Royal, but I know what you mean."

I don't react. Starling can try all he wants, but he's never getting in good with me.

Julep crosses to give Haru a hug. "This smells amazing. Thank you for making it." She turns back toward us. "I'll be right back. I've got to unload." She gestures over her whole body.

I watch Julep for a second before pushing back my chair and following her through the den and into the armory. If she's been training Starling, maybe she can fill me in on him a little. Unlike Royal, she'll probably be willing to give me her impression of the new guy.

Once inside the armory, Julep uses her palm print to unlock her gun safe, and systematically unloads two handguns, a handful of clips, and two tactical knives. The amount of gear that woman carries concealed on her body is awe-inspiring.

Her eyes catch sight of me grinning at her and smiles back. "What can I say?" She locks her safe and walks back down the hall toward the kitchen.

With one hand, I tap her arm. "Hold on a sec." I angle my body away from the kitchen, my back against the wall.

Julep moves toward me, leaning in. "What?"

"You've been training Starling?"

She nods. "Yes, ma'am. For the past four months."

Four months. My stomach drops. Royal must not have wasted any time after Vale died to start searching for a replacement. Only, Vale can't be replaced, and especially not by that brown-noser sitting in the kitchen.

I slide my hands into the pockets of my trench coat. "Do you think he'll be a good addition to the team?"

She tilts her head, chewing the inside of her lip as she does so. She glances over her shoulder toward the kitchen before meeting my eyes. "Honestly? We could use him. He's got a great tactical mind, great marksman, good in close-quarters combat… Plus he's a team player. I think you'll like him if you give him the chance."

My gaze slides toward the kitchen before turning back to Julep. "If you say so."

"I do, and look." Julep puts a hand on my shoulder. "I know you've been bottling your emotions since Vale died—"

I open my mouth to cut her off, like I have every other time she's brought this up over the past few months, but Julep holds her other hand up to silence me. "Don't interrupt."

A frown rises to my mouth, but I remain quiet.

"You've been struggling. The whole team knows. Maybe Starling can give you a kick in the pants, or whatever it is you

36

need." She winks at me.

My eyes narrow in a scowl at the implication, but Julep is already gliding away from me into the kitchen, chuckling softly.

I do not need a kick in the pants. Or anything else. And especially not from Starling.

# Chapter 7

Haru has already carried the two large, sizzling woks to the table and put them on hot pads when I return to the kitchen.

Julep is sitting across the table from Lotus, leaving me two choices—sit kitty-corner to Starling, or across from him. Great. I choose the seat across from him. It'll be fairly easy to keep my eyes on my plate so I don't have to look at 6' of not-Vale.

Haru sits kitty-corner to me at the other end of the table. "Dig in!" She motions toward the tongs she's positioned in the woks. She doesn't have to tell us twice.

Lotus grabs the tongs and dishes himself a huge portion of teriyaki chicken and noodles.

Clarity, on the other hand, goes for the version dotted with tiny squares of tofu. Once she's done, she holds the tongs out to Starling.

"No thanks. I mean, tofu is fine, but I'd rather have the teriyaki." He bites his lip in embarrassment. "Sorry, Haru."

"No problem," she chirps. "I'm a vegetarian so I always make both."

"That's how we do it," Lotus adds. "We each take a meal,

and we pretty much all do two versions. That way we can all eat together. Break bread, catch up, all that."

Starling nods. "That sounds great. When is it my turn?"

Julep laughs. "Can you cook?"

"Sure. Pancakes, mac and cheese… I admit my aunt did most of the cooking."

"Your aunt?" Haru asks through a mouthful of tofu noodles.

"My aunt raised me. My dad was always gone for work. And my mom died when I was two."

"That's awful," Clarity whispers, her eyes bouncing to me and back to Starling's face.

Don't say it. I will the command in Clarity's direction, thinking as loudly as I can.

Clarity takes a bite of noodles and chews slowly. "She sounds lovely," my sister says, her heavy brown eyes watching me.

"So, where are all of your parents?" Starling looks around the room at each of us, an open smile on his face.

It makes me want to smack him, this bright-eyed curiosity he's got. Still, there isn't a lot my teammates can give away by answering the question, so I bite my tongue.

"Don't have any," Lotus says. "Royal pulled me out of foster care a few years ago."

"I'm sorry," Starling says, voice quiet. "I bet it was difficult."

Lotus shrugs. "Some placements are great, and some not so much."

The new guy frowns.

"It's no big deal," Lotus says, elbowing Starling lightly on the arm. "Don't sweat it."

Starling gives a slow nod. "And you, Clarity?"

"They passed when I was small," Clarity says. "Royal is my adopted father."

"That makes Loveday your sister?" Starling asks.

"Yes," Clarity says with a smile. "A great one."

I wink at her.

"And you?" Starling looks at Haru, waiting for her response.

"They're back in..." She stops, and a wistful, sad look flits across her face. "I'm not supposed to say, am I?"

I give a shake of my head.

Haru gives me a grateful smile and turns back to Starling. "Royal promised my parents he'd give me a good education here in the United States. It was the only way my mom would let me come."

"Do you talk to them often?" Starling leans toward her, listening intently.

"I haven't talked to my mom in months, but I talk to my dad some." She stares down at her plate. An uncomfortable silence falls over the table as Haru fidgets in her seat.

"Enough about that," I say gruffly. With a finger, I tap my watch to open the weather app. It's raining out now, but it's supposed to stop in the next couple hours. "Eat up because we're going out to the jungle for training tonight. Capture the flag. We'll meet at the armory at 20:00."

"Capture the flag?" Starling asks, eyes alight.

"Once it gets dark, we go out to the stand of trees behind the hotel, split into two teams, and play," Lotus says. "One team guards the flag while the other team tries to steal it."

"It helps us with strategy, communication, and team building," Haru says. They're the exact words I used to describe it to her the first time she played. A smile lifts at the memory of her first game, when her enthusiasm, and subsequent excited squeaks, made her an easy target. She'll never be a field agent, but she's a cracking computer guru.

"And it's fun." Julep grins after swallowing her bite of noodles.

"Sounds awesome." Starling takes another forkful from his plate, chews, and swallows. "Does Royal play?"

Lotus cackles. "No, Son. We'll train with him starting tomorrow. Loveday runs the night games."

"That's right," I say. "Tonight your asses are mine." Okay, that sounded a little strong, even for me, but I let it hang in the air.

Clarity eyes me, one eyebrow raised, but says nothing.

"Yes, ma'am," Starling says, unfazed by my statement. Right, the military background.

"What are the teams?" Julep asks.

I study each of my teammates before resting my gaze on Starling. "Let's see what you've got. You, Haru, and Julep will start with the flag. Clarity, Lotus, and I will try to steal it." I've put him at a disadvantage by putting Haru on his team. I'm curious to see how he'll handle it in the field, because sometimes we go into a job at a disadvantage, whether we know it or not.

Starling cracks a wide smile. "It'll be my pleasure."

The jungle is going to be sopping wet after the rain. Tonight is going to get a little messy.

41

# Chapter 8

I'm just stepping into the dormitory hallway to change for capture the flag when, at the end of the hall, Julep steps out of Lotus's room, a smile on her face. When she locks eyes with me, she pauses and her mouth opens to say something.

My eyebrows lift.

Then she's walking forward again, her body relaxed as she moves. "I was just asking him about conditions out there, since I haven't played with you guys in a few months."

"Fraternizing with the enemy?" I ask.

"There was no fraternizing of any kind," she says, running her fingers down one of her braids.

I chuckle at her serious demeanor. "I was kidding."

"Oh." Her lips curve upward.

Is it just me, or is she relieved? That idea sets my wheels turning. "See you in a bit," I say.

"Yep," she says, ducking into her room and closing the door behind her.

I stride up the hallway and tap on Lotus's doorframe. He's at the back of his room, arranging his shot glasses.

His eyes light when he catches sight of me. "Look what Julep brought me back from London." With careful fingers, he picks up a shot glass and holds it out for me to see.

I cross the room and take it from him, admiring the tiny London Eye printed on the glass. "It's cute."

"What have I told you about the word, 'cute?'" he says, taking the shot glass from me and replacing it on the shelf.

"Right. It's super macho," I say. And for good measure, I throw in a grunt.

"You're the worst."

Before I can react, he lunges, gripping me in a headlock and messing up my hair.

Our laughter echoes up the hall, until I reach my inside arm toward his face to bend his head backward.

He fights against me, threatening to bite my outstretched fingers. And that's why he doesn't see what I'm doing with my inside knee.

My knee meets the backside of his, Lotus's inside foot flies out from under him. In a blink, he's on the ground, looking up at me. "Damn," he says, laughing. "That's cold."

I reach out a hand to help him up. "Maybe we should do some sparing here soon."

"Maybe." His eyes meet mine as he reaches up and pats his afro. "You needed something?"

In my peripheral vision, I can see the shot glasses lined up neatly along the wooden shelf. "Nope. Just wanted to see if you were almost ready."

He gestures over the all black clothing he's wearing, from his shoes up to his black tee. "Do I look ready?"

"You do."

"Cool." He nods and I turn away.

"See you in a few." I toss the words over my shoulder as I

take the few steps to my own door. In my head, my wheels are turning. Julep brought Lotus a gift back from London, something she knew would be important to him. As far as I know, she's never brought Royal, Clarity, or Haru gifts. I chew the inside of my cheek. It's an interesting development, to say the least.

Clarity is in our room, already dressed, and reading on her mattress on the floor.

I rummage through my dresser and change quickly. Yanking the zipper on my hoodie closed, I turn to Clarity. "We have to win tonight."

My sister looks up from her book. "What are you so worried about?" She unfolds from her cross-legged position and puts her feet into the combat boots she's chosen for our excursion. "You've been on edge all day."

My fingers scratch at my scalp under my icy blonde hair. "Starling."

Clarity narrows her eyes, taking in my hunched shoulders and clenched fists. "You're still worried that Dad brought him here to replace you."

Hearing it from my sister's mouth is a shock to my system. I look away, studying the bland gray carpet. "Yes."

Clarity stands and glides across the room toward me. How she is able to do that in combat boots I can't figure out. "Dad would never replace you. You're his daughter. And our fearless leader." She gives me half a smile and tweaks my chin.

"Thanks," I say, pulling her into a hug.

"Have you noticed how similar he is to Vale?" she whispers into my ear.

I break our embrace and turn my back. "He is nothing like Vale."

She moves around me and hovers within an arm's length.

"He's exactly like Vale."

He *is* exactly like Vale. Calm, capable, and eager to be part of a team. I spin around to face her, punctuating my words with my hands. "No one is replacing Vale." Or me. I look at my watch. It's nearly 20:00. "Let's go."

Clarity squeezes my shoulder and leads me down the hall, through the den to the armory, where everyone is waiting.

Including Charles Darnay, who stands in the center of the room wearing relaxed-fit jeans, a black turtleneck, and a crisp, black peacoat.

What is he doing here? I step forward into the semi-circle my teenaged teammates have formed around Darnay. He is gesturing with his hands, mimicking a gun being fired. "So we were pinned down. I didn't have any full clips left. And Royal, he was bleeding pretty badly. We just knew that that was it. We were going to die. And then, some little old lady comes up the stairs, surprises the bad guy, and tasers him. It was hilarious. We almost died from laughter. And then, of course, we got out of there." He is laughing so hard tears start to run down his cheeks and into his neatly trimmed beard. He wipes at his face quickly. "Sorry about that. Hazard of the job. Have to laugh when you can."

"How many times have you been shot?" Haru asks, eyeing him and looking horrified. Her black hair is swept back into a ponytail that dusts her shoulders, and her bangs are pushed to one side.

"Only four or five. Not as many as you would think." He winks at her.

She blushes and looks away.

I fight the urge to grimace. The false modesty he's putting off is odiously repellant. I glance around. Everyone else seems to be buying it. Julep is leaning toward him, smiling. Clearly there are no hard feelings between her and her former boss. Lotus is scratching at the back of his neck, something he does when he's nervous. Clarity is watching Darnay wide-eyed. Starling is standing off to one side, mouth open, his black v-neck giving just a glimpse of collarbone beneath his unzipped hoodie.

Focus, Loveday. I clear my throat. "We were just on our way out," I say.

"I know," Darnay grins. "Lotus told me you guys were going paintballing. Mind if I join?"

"It's a training exercise."

"I don't think your dad would mind. I promise to stay out of the way." He gives me an over-wide, fake grin.

I frown, thinking it over. "Fine, but don't interfere." I move past him to the far end of the armory and open the door to the metal cage where we keep the paintball gear. We don't keep this one locked since nothing inside is lethal. One by one, I hand out our guns, pistols, paintballs, and goggles. Lastly I grab the flag. Actually, it's not a flag. It's a battered, paint-splattered, miniature Eiffel Tower that Julep brought back from a trip to Vegas. Since she's a few years older than the rest of us, twenty-four to our sixteen to nineteen, Royal lets her go on solo trips when we have easy jobs. I can't wait to be old enough for that, but it'll be a couple years before Royal will allow it.

"Everyone ready?" I push through to the front of the group. "Holster your pistols. Keep your guns down until we get out of the parking lot. We don't want to scare the guests." I stow my paint pistol on my left hip and hold my larger paintball gun down at my right side. The goggles are stashed in the front pocket of my hoodie.

We walk through the den, pushing past its worn chairs and couch, and down the short hallway that's lit only by tube lights along the floor, up to an intricate electrical panel. I stand still long enough for the facial recognition software to scan my face. Once it authenticates my features, the panel beeps and the large metal door slides into the wall.

I step out of the Ivory Tower and into the hotel's service tunnel. It's a long, dank concrete tunnel with pipes running along the ceiling. A string of metal pendant lights hangs from above, creating spots of bright light in the gloom. A heavy breath escapes me. It's warm and sticky in here.

We walk down the hallway and unlock the door to the parking lot. It spits us out in a dark corner of the hotel's underground parking garage. The door creaks shut behind us. On the outside, the door is dented and scratched, and the paint is peeling in spots. Anyone who noticed the door would think it was long abandoned.

In the parking garage, the asphalt is striped with wet tire tracks, and several of the parked cars glisten with droplets of rainwater.

I stop at the edge of the parking garage to check the small above-ground parking lot. There isn't anyone in sight, probably due to the late afternoon rain.

I lead everyone across to the green space behind the hotel. We slide down the grassy slope toward the drainage ditch. The heavy scent of rain-soaked grass fills my nostrils. In a clump, we move toward the gaping maw of the tunnel that leads under the street. A plastic soda bottle crunches under my foot, its loud crunch jarring in the still night air. On the other side of the tunnel, the stars are beginning to peek out from behind their cloudy curtain, their tiny twinklings dotting the navy sky. A grove of red maple and scarlet oak trees begins at the bottom of the hill and marches up to the top. I duck under low-hanging branches as I weave between the thick trunks of the trees.

Once I crest the hill, I stop at the treeline. Below me, Washington, D.C., stretches out in an expanse of light. I turn to my teammates. Beside me, Clarity huffs into her hands.

"Did you bring gloves?" I ask.

"I should have," she says. "It's freezing out here."

Without a word, Starling pulls off the black gloves he's wearing and holds them out to her. When her eyes move from the gloves to his face, he smiles. "I don't need them."

My sister beams at him and takes the gloves, pulling them onto her hands. "Thank you."

"You're welcome."

Starling turns his gaze to me, his deep-set brown eyes looking dark in the gloom.

"You ready?" I ask.

He nods.

"Good. You and your team will start here, guarding the flag." I hand over the Eiffel Tower. "Good luck."

At this, Darnay peels off from the group and fades into the trees, not saying a word. I don't know where he's going, so I focus on my teammates for the game.

"Clarity, Lotus, come on." I walk back down the hill, my sneakers sticking in the mud. Lotus stomps along behind me. Clarity's footsteps are silent, as always.

Once I get back to the tunnel, I stop and turn to Clarity. "Lotus and I will flank the hill and try for the flag. You provide backup."

She smiles. "I can handle that."

"Which side of the hill do you want?" Lotus asks. "It's pretty slick out there."

"I'll take the far side."

"Let's do this," he says, pumping his paintball gun.

I pull my black beanie out of my pocket and tug it down

over my platinum hair. Next I put on my night goggles and scan the hill. Haru is at the top of the rise, crouched behind a log, guarding the flag. I don't see Julep or Starling. "You guys ready for this?"

"It's going to be fun," Lotus chuckles.

Behind me, I can hear Clarity loading her paintball pistol.

I walk through the mud as quietly as I can, but it's not easy to do. Each step results in a low squashing sound as the mud suctions to my tennis shoes. The whirr of road noise covers some of it, but even so this is going to be tricky.

A smile flits across my face. Last time we played in the mud we all got filthy. Both bathrooms looked like a mud monster had died in there afterward.

With my night goggles in place, it's easy to scan the hill. Haru hasn't moved, but now I can see Julep as well. She's on Lotus's side of the hill. That should be entertaining. I stand still where I am behind a tree, wondering who will get taken down first. My money is on Lotus.

Starling is still nowhere to be seen, so I creep along, using trees or fallen logs to shelter my way. My heart starts to pound. There's more riding on this game than I care to admit.

And then I hear the rapid clicking sound of a paintball gun firing.

A mangled yell filters over the hill.

**Lotus**
**I'm out.**

Yep. Not surprised. He's a killer driver, but not the stealthiest of people. My back presses into the tree behind me, the ripples of bark pushing through my hoodie. Deep breaths. I can do this. It helps to remember that Clarity is out here somewhere, spooky silent like a ghost.

I scan my surroundings and finally spot Starling. He's holed up behind a giant tree stump off near the top of the hill. His head is moving side to side as he searches the area. He has no idea where I am. Perfect. It's time to make a move, and I'll make one all right. I'm going to sneak up behind him and shoot him.

I loop down and around the hill as quietly as I can, but no matter how slowly I move I still make small noises. Brittle twigs crack every few steps, and the snap is so loud I might as well announce my location. A cricket silences its chirping as I approach.

Starling is still behind the log.

I step on a twig and it cracks loudly, splitting the air.

On the other side of the hill, another paintball gun is fired. Instinct makes me duck even though the sound isn't that close by.

No message comes through on my watch, so if anyone is out, it's probably Julep. Assuming I'm right, that would leave Haru, Starling, Clarity, and me still in play.

The hairs on the back of my neck stand on end as I sense someone behind me. I whirl around.

Clarity is standing five feet away, her gun at the ready.

"Julep?" I mouth.

A sly smile comes to my sister's face, and she holds up her pistol.

I pump my fist.

She tilts head toward the top of the hill. I nod and lead her up. Fat drops of rainwater fall from the trees above us, dappling our black clothes.

Silently, we flank Haru. I fire one well-aimed shot that hits her in the back.

She lets out a shrill squeal before hunching over and typing something into her watch. Then she straightens and picks her way toward the bottom of the hill.

Clarity sneaks forward and picks up the Eiffel Tower.

"Let's get down the hill," I whisper.

A branch swishes to our left. I spin around and shoot in that direction but don't hear the sounds of impact. I must have missed.

Paintballs come flying toward me from behind a tree. I jump out of the way, but one of them grazes my leg. Shit. I land flat on my stomach in the mud with a smack. The thick mud oozes through my knit pants and sticks the fabric to my skin. I groan as I push myself up to a sitting position. My gun is covered in mud, and so is my front, from my shoes up to my neck. I managed to keep my face out of it, but that's about it.

To my left, a paintball pistol is fired.

Starling lets out a laugh.

Clarity steps out from behind the tree holding the Eiffel Tower in one hand and her pistol in the other. "Team Loveday wins," she calls cheerily.

Lotus lets out a whoop from the bottom of the hill.

From where we're standing, Haru's chattering is barely audible, not much more than a murmur of words as she talks to Lotus. I strain to hear what she's saying, but it's no use. I'm too far away. I'm missing something, but what?

Then it hits me—Darnay is out here somewhere.

I whip around, reaching for Clarity. "Watch out!"

It's too late. Clarity lunges forward as paintballs hit her squarely in the back of the head.

Darnay steps out from behind a tree and takes the Eiffel Tower from her fingers. "It looks like I win." He grins and raises the icon. "This was fun. We should do it again sometime." He tosses the tower to me and brushes past on his way down the hill, chuckling.

Annoyance and grudging respect rise in my chest. Maybe he's not a total buffoon after all.

# Chapter 9

Dread at the day's training wakes me earlier than normal and I roll out of bed, falling the few feet to the floor and landing ungracefully on my heels.

"Morning," Clarity says without looking at me. She's drawing fake hairs on her chin with a sharpened eyeliner pencil.

"New look?" I ask.

"Yep," she responds without her eyes leaving the mirror.

"Awesome." I get ready for the day and head to the kitchen. A breakfast burrito sounds fantastic this morning.

I'm sitting at the long table at the back of the control room, my hands cupping a piping hot burrito when Starling enters. He meets my eyes and smiles before sliding into the chair across from me. "Paintball was awesome last night."

"Yes."

"Clarity really got me."

"She does that."

"She is freaky quiet. How does she do that?"

I shrug. "Ask her." My emphasis on the second word, and my brusque manner, stop him cold.

Starling opens his mouth to speak, but then focuses on his hands, which are folded in his lap.

Lotus saunters in with his bike helmet under his arm. "You missed a killer sunrise."

I smirk. "You know what's not awesome? The traffic you probably had to sit in this morning."

"Worth it." He holds his fist out to Starling, who responds in kind. They fist bump.

Haru skips into the room and plops down at her desk. She whips open her laptop and starts typing away, her eyes meeting mine for a split second. Since she moved down into the Ivory Tower a month ago, I've contemplated filling her in on what Vale had been trying to do with Royal's laptop before he died. Yet, something's been holding me back. If it's not bothering Clarity, maybe I should just leave it alone. I never got any notifications from the software Vale installed, so whatever information Royal has in Clarity's file may yet remain a secret.

Lotus walks over and sits beside Haru. He whispers something in her ear and she giggles.

Starling leans toward me. "Are they...?" he whispers.

I shake my head. "No. He was the first person she connected with when we met her, so they're pretty close."

Footsteps sound in the hallway and I turn toward the door. Clarity swaggers in, dressed as a guy. She's rocking a shaggy, brunette wig, baggy jeans, and a navy-blue men's waffle Henley. Even the way she walks is altered. She's finally mastered a man's walk, and confidence oozes from her. A glance at her neck reveals that she's even done some clever shading to make it appear that she has an Adam's apple. She sits on the couch, legs wide, arms spread across its back.

Starling stands quickly. "Morning," he says. "We haven't met yet." He crosses the room with his hand extended.

The tinkling of Clarity's laugh fills the room.

Starling turns to me, his face contorted in confusion. "Is this?"

I laugh. "Clarity."

He lets out a chuckle. "That's impressive. So, this is your thing?"

Clarity gives him a nod, looking pleased. "Disguises? Yes."

Starling returns to his chair across from me and sits, shaking his head. "She really got me."

"You have no idea," I say.

"The first time I saw her she was dressed as a hunched over, wrinkly old woman," Lotus adds. "I thought she was about ninety years old. Hearing her voice was jarring."

Starling nods. "I bet."

Royal enters, followed by Darnay. "I read your report about your training last night," he says to me. "It sounds like it went well."

I nod, the image of Darnay with his gun aimed at my sister still fresh in my mind. "It did."

"Let's get started, shall we?" Royal interrupts. He and Darnay sit at the table with Starling and me. "We'll start today at the gun range, and then come back here for some team building." He gives Darnay a knowing smile.

The sight of it creeps me out. Something tells me I am not going to like whatever he has planned.

I use my palm to unlock my gun safe and survey my weapons. I'm trying to decide between my M16 and my Sig Sauer MCX Rattler when Starling appears in my peripheral vision. Royal has assigned him the safe next to mine. Vale's safe.

I grab my M16 and my Glock 17, a few extra clips, and stow them in my rifle bag. I slam my safe closed and stomp out of the armory. Adding someone to the team without consulting me is bad enough, but his obvious attempts to replace Vale make my stomach churn. I shoot a glare at Royal as I brush past. He watches me pass, a frown etched into his features. I'm already on thin ice, but I just don't even care.

Each of us totes a rifle bag as we tromp through the service tunnel to the parking lot. I take a moment to let my eyes adjust to the glare from the harsh morning sun.

Royal's black fifteen-passenger van sits in the back corner of the lot.

We carefully stack our bags in the back of the van before piling in. I crawl into the back of the vehicle and Clarity follows me. We sit together in the middle two seats that make up the back row, leaving the two outside seats unoccupied. She leans her head back against the headrest and closes her eyes. If she had it her way we'd start exercises closer to 12:00 than 08:00.

Lotus and Haru climb into the seats directly in front of us. He slings his arm across the back of the seat.

"My hair!" Haru squeaks, pulling her stick straight ponytail out from under Lotus's extended arm.

"Oops," he says before relaxing his arm onto the back of the seat again.

Julep sits on the aisle next to Haru. Curious, I lean over and catch a glimpse of a knife hilt sticking out of her boot. Then I sit back in my seat, mimicking Clarity's reclined position. Unlike my sister, I keep my eyes open slits, observing the goings on inside the van.

Lotus, trying to be sneaky, snatches a look at Julep as she's fastening her seatbelt. So that's how it is? He's obviously got romantic feelings for her, and I'm inclined to think she feels the same way about him, if that shot glass she gave him is any indication. It's something I'll have to keep an eye on because of Royal's strict "no dating" policy. Of course, it didn't stop Vale and me. A smile flits across my face.

Starling is the last to climb into the van. He shoots a long look toward where Clarity and I are sitting in the back, but scoots into the front middle row directly behind the driver's seat instead. He swings the van doors closed and buckles himself in.

Royal turns to look at us while Darnay arranges himself in the passenger seat. "Everyone ready?"

A chorus of affirmative responses bubbles up from the back of the van, so he turns to face front and pulls out of the lot.

I put my Bluetooth headphone in one ear and hold the other one up for Clarity.

"No thanks," she murmurs, closing her eyes again.

I only offered to be polite. She hates the metal I listen to now. Vale's music. I push a button on my watch and loud, angry music filters into my ears.


Half an hour later we're standing in the parking lot looking up at a corrugated metal building. Faded, white painted letters over the door proclaim the place to be the home of Mo's Lawn Mower Repair Shop. A sign in the dingy front window reads, "Closed." A plane rumbles overhead toward the air force base.

Royal opens the back of the van and Clarity hands out our bags.

"Mo's Lawn Mower Repair Shop?" Starling reads slowly, his head cocked to the side.

Julep grins. "The inside should look familiar."

"Oh, got it," Starling says, his eyes skimming the warehouse. There's a glimmer of confidence in his expression that wasn't there a minute ago.

"Follow me," Royal says. He strides toward the door of the gray metal structure, unlocking it with a quick scan of his palm and motioning us in. Once we are all inside, he locks the door behind us by inputting a code into an alarm panel. Then he flips a switch to turn on the lights. Slowly, the industrial pendant lights come on, illuminating the building's ample space. To our left, there is a gun range set up with six booths across. We'll have to take turns shooting if Royal and Darnay intend to put in some practice time.

On the other side of the warehouse there are some dummy walls set up on rollers. We use it for practicing infiltrating structures. I'm not sure what Royal has in mind for today.

He turns to us and speaks. "We'll take turns in the booths at the gun range. Those who are not shooting will practice cat-and-mouse using the dummy panels." He pats Darnay on the shoulder. "Charles has agreed to supervise at the gun range while I oversee the cat-and-mouse exercises."

A smile turns up the corners of my mouth. Sweet. Cat-and-mouse is my favorite, mostly because I almost never lose. And by that I mean I've lost to Clarity a handful of times in as many years.

But today isn't my day. First Clarity beats me, and then it takes me way too long to nail Lotus.

"Loveday, get your head in the game," Royal says to me, arms crossed over his wrinkle-free, burgundy button-up shirt. "Starling, you're next. See if you can beat your team leader."

Starling turns to me, eyes lit. "Yes, sir." He advances toward me, a hesitant smile on his lips. He whispers, "Before we start, I want you to know that Lotus told me about your mom. I'm sorry."

I bristle. "And that's supposed to affect my performance somehow?"

Starling's eyes widen and his mouth drops. "No, no, I just meant that I know, and I'm sorry. I wasn't trying to psych you out."

I huff. "Whatever. It was a long time ago." My voice is rough, and I refuse to meet his eyes. Instead, I scan the warehouse, checking the progress of my teammates. Haru, Clarity, and Julep are all at the gun range, Haru watching the other two unload their weapons onto the bench that runs the length of the range. Beside them, Darnay is preparing his guns. I wonder what he carries?

Starling bites his lip, then tries a different tack. "Are you ready for this?" He smiles again, wider this time. "I really enjoyed playing it with Julep. I got pretty good at it."

My eyes narrow at this. It's definitely a challenge. "You're on."

I walk into the maze of dummy walls and crouch in a corner, waiting for Starling to advance. All I have to do is hit him with the paintball gun before he shoots me, and I win. The catch is that as the mouse I have to remain in one place for thirty seconds before I can move. The restriction makes me a target for Starling, whose movement isn't limited once he's within the bounds of the maze. I set a silent alarm on my watch and wait, my heart pounding. I take controlled breaths through my nose to keep myself calm, just like I've been trained to do.

Behind me, the wall wavers, and I bend toward the floor to sneak a peek underneath it. Starling is there, moving in slow, steady steps, his paintball gun at the ready. He's just around the corner, and I can't move for another eight seconds. I sit up and scan the area, thinking fast as the seconds drag on.

Six seconds.

Five

Four

Three

My legs itch to move, to run to safety, but I have to abide by the rules of the game. I'm fuming at the thought of being bested by Starling during his first cat-and-mouse game, when his steps move in the other direction, and my watch vibrates. It's time for me to move. I stand, straining to hear noises over the loud pops of gunfire from the gun range. Nearby, a wheel squeaks, and I freeze, my back to the wall and my gun at the ready.

He's not going to beat me. Not now, and not ever.

# Chapter 10

"I can't believe Starling got the drop on you," Lotus crows at the dinner table. "I've never seen anyone best you. Not even Vale."

Clarity reaches over and puts a hand on his. When he meets her eyes, she gives a slight shake of her head.

Lotus shrinks back at the glare I give him, and focuses on the vegetarian lasagna on his plate.

My fork twirls in my fingers as I stare at my half-eaten food. I can't believe it either. Cat-and-mouse is my game. Or it was, until today. I'm disgusted with myself.

"It's no big deal," Starling says, sneaking a look at me. "Everyone has off days. I got lucky." But he can't stop grinning as he speaks. He is, no doubt, basking in the glow of having beaten his team leader.

"Loveday," Royal says. I spin to meet his eyes. He's standing at the foot of the stairway into the kitchen, thumbs hooked into the pockets of his slacks. "Come with me."

I swallow the bite of lasagna that's tucked into my cheek, push back my chair, and follow him down the hall, through the den into the control room.

"Have a seat," he says, gesturing a hand toward Haru's desk.

"I'm fine standing."

Royal gives me an appraising look before nodding. "Very well."

"What's going on? Do we have a new mission?"

"This isn't about that."

My body tenses, and I cross my arms over my chest.

"This is about you and your performance over the past six months."

I lick my lips. This isn't going to be good. "Dad, I—"

"Don't interrupt," he says. "I know you had a hard time after Vale died. It was a horrible experience, kneeling in the middle of the road with him bleeding out in front of you." He closes his eyes and pinches the bridge of his nose for a moment, then he opens them again and levels them at me. "I've been waiting for you to bounce back, not emotionally, but mentally, physically. It hasn't happened. I'm worried that if I put you in the field, if we go after The Chin, that you will get hurt because of your reduced performance. I'm not sure what to do about it."

"So you had Julep train Starling. As my replacement." The word catches on my tongue and comes out cracked and gravelly.

He nods slowly.

One good thing about Royal is that if you ask a straightforward question, you will get a straightforward answer.

"I don't want to take you out of the field." His clear blue eyes are stern, focused.

"You're as good an agent as any I've worked with, but I will do it if it's necessary. Your safety is more important to me than your ego. I will be watching you closely tomorrow, to see if you can get your form back. If you can't…"

"You'll what? Lock me in my room?" I throw a hand up in the air in the general direction of the dormitory.

"Don't be childish," he says. "Charles has agreed to allow you to work at the concierge desk for the hotel, if necessary."

I grit my teeth. That would be worse than being locked in my room.

"Do we understand each other?"

"Yes, sir." I emphasize the second word as if it were a dagger in my hand.

Royal's eyes widen at the venom in my response. He studies me for a moment before speaking. "I'm truly sorry about Vale. He was a great young man. I know you two were close."

An image of Vale and myself, hiding from Clarity behind a shower curtain, clothed only in hot steam from the running water, settles in my mind's eye. I swallow the lump in my throat, spin on my heel, and retreat to the dormitory.

I've got to be careful. I can't play sloppy. If I do Royal *will* replace me. Whatever he has planned for our training exercises tomorrow, I have to nail it.


"Morning everyone," Royal says. He stands at the front of the control room in a gray button-up, charcoal slacks, and black loafers. Darnay stands beside him in a navy houndstooth jacket, maroon button-up, khaki pants, and brown loafers. He has his hands behind his back.

I raise an eyebrow. They're up to something.

"It's our last day of training before team selection," Royal says. "I need to see your best today. That includes your physical and mental abilities. It is vital that you work as a team. I have

63

quite the challenge planned for you this morning." He turns to Darnay with a sliver of a smile on his lips. "Charles?"

Darnay steps forward and produces a handful of blindfolds from behind his back.

"What are those for?" I ask with eyes narrowed.

"You'll see," Royal says. He looks at me, his face somber. "I need your best today, Loveday."

My hackles rise and I clench my jaw. It's a power move, calling me out in front of our entire team. A challenge. I want to argue with him that I give my best every day, but since Vale died, it wouldn't be the truth. I've lost my edge and I don't know if I'll be able to find it.

"Follow me." He motions with one arm and leads us through the den and down a narrow hallway to the small training room/bunker we use here in the Ivory Tower. He turns to face us. "Each of you will wear a blindfold," he says.

Darnay hands them out.

The charcoal black blindfold is cool and soft in my hand, but the idea of covering my eyes goes against all of my instincts. My sight, my ability to observe, is vital in this line of work. If I can't see, how will I protect myself and my teammates? I shove down the rising panic and focus on my surroundings. I have to stay mentally sharp, or I'm done. And the idea of wearing one of those stupid employee vests and a nametag makes me want to hurl. Nametags are my nemesis. They're too obvious, and being put in a situation where someone knows my name before I know anything about them makes me squirm.

Haru and Lotus are already blindfolded. Clarity moves close to me, holding her blindfold out. Her natural hair, wavy and brunette, is tousled to one side and skims her jawline. She's dressed in a cream colored waffle short-sleeved shirt and olive green slacks. No matter what my sister is wearing, she looks effortless, which is a blatant falsehood. I've seen how much work she puts into her look each day.

I take Clarity's blindfold and move behind her to tie it over her eyes, being careful not to pull the strands of hair that twine around the fabric. Reaching down, I take her hand and put it on my shoulder so she can follow me.

"You too, Loveday," Royal says.

I stare at him for a beat. "Fine."

Starling is tying a scarf over Julep's eyes. Once he is finished he turns to me. "I can tie yours too," he offers.

Grudgingly, I nod and turn my back to him. He takes the blindfold from my hand and gingerly places it over my eyes. Strands of my bleached blonde hair pull against my scalp as he ties the scarf securely in place. My body shudders when his fingers brush the back of my neck.

"Thanks," I mutter.

"You're welcome," he whispers back.

The rubbing of fabric behind me alerts me to movement. I assume that Darnay has stepped forward to tie Starling's blindfold.

"Good luck," Darnay says, barely able to contain his glee.

"Thanks," Starling returns, his voice tight. From the sound of it, he isn't any more a fan of this exercise than I am.

Royal speaks next. "Charles and I will lead you into the bunker. Once you are inside, wait for my instructions."

The bunker door creaks open. A large hand takes mine. "Follow me." Royal propels me forward over the threshold into the bunker, and Clarity follows, her hand still on my shoulder. He guides my hand to a rough, partially frayed rope. It's strung tight so that it runs parallel to the floor at waist height. "Grab hold of this."

My fingers wrap around the cord and I focus on the sensation of the wiry fibers against my skin. What is Royal up to? Whatever it is, he hasn't ever used this training exercise on me before.

The rise and fall of footsteps around me signals the arrival of my teammates in the room.

After a few minutes of shuffling, Royal speaks again. "Your task is to escape this maze by working as a team. You may communicate with each other by any means. There is one rule: you each must have one hand on the rope at all times. If both of your hands leave the rope you will be removed from the exercise. Once you have found the exit, Charles will tap you on the shoulder. After this happens, you are to remain silent. Any questions?"

"No," I say. "We've got it."

The bunker door thuds closed.

Royal's voice comes through our earbuds. "You may remove the blindfolds."

With my right hand, I reach up and pull the cloth off, careful not to take my other hand off the rope. Darkness envelops me. Even without the blindfold on, the bunker is pitch black. I squint my eyes, looking for something, anything, and finally find a small, blinking red light above me. It must be from a camera. Royal is surveilling us from outside the room.

I stand completely still and listen to the sounds in the room, but it's silent. There don't appear to be any electronic obstacles set up, but I can't be too careful. Even though it's dark, I can do this. I've been training for surprises like this since I was twelve. "Here is what we are going to do," I say. "First, let's all find each other. Okay?"

A chorus of affirmative responses reaches my ears. "Good. Everyone remain where you are until I reach you." I shuffle forward, skimming the ground with my feet so as not to trip over any possible obstacles, and bump into Julep.

"Oof."

"Sorry," I say, trying to sound confident. "Put your hand on my shoulder and follow me." I turn around and move in the opposite direction, careful to keep one hand on the rope the entire time. After only a few steps, I run headlong into Starling, who lets out a low chuckle.

"Sorry," he says.

"No problem." Starling in front. Julep behind. I could let one of them lead, but Royal said he needed my best, and I'm best when I'm calling the shots. "Let me pass you." The frayed fibers of the rope course along my palm as I skim the rope, feeling for Starling's hand. Royal said I had to keep my hand on the rope at all times, but he didn't say I had to keep all of my fingers on it. I tap the back of Starling's hand with my pointer. "Be still while I move around you."

He tenses as I reach past him for the rope, ducking under his extended arm and rising on his other side. "Julep, put a hand on Starling's shoulder. Starling, follow me."

He puts a light hand on my shoulder and waits for me to move forward.

"Roll call," I say.

"I'm here," Haru says, followed by Clarity and Lotus. Judging by their voices, Haru is closest.

"Haru, where are you again?"

Her voice sounds from a few feet away. "Over here."

I move toward her, following the rope.

After a few awkward minutes of shuffling backward and forward along the rope in the dark, we manage to find Haru, then Lotus, and, lastly, Clarity.

"So, what's the plan?" Lotus asks in the dark.

I scan the room again. "I can't see anything in here besides the red light from the camera in the ceiling. Does anyone else see anything?"

A chorus of responses in the negative greets my ears.

"Does anyone hear anything?" I stand still, straining my ears for any sound, but the only vibrations that reach my ears are the breaths of my teammates and the quiet brushes of fabric in motion.

"Does anyone smell anything?" Again I stand motionless, breathing in deeply.

Down the line, Lotus inhales. "Julep smells like… sweet red plums and grilled cheese sandwiches."

There's a light smack of flesh against flesh.

"Ouch. Don't hate."

"That's what I ate for lunch, ding-a-ling."

I shake my head before realizing that it's pointless. My teammates can't see me. "Focus, everyone. Royal said this was a maze, so let's walk through it and find the exit." Clarity and Haru are in front, Starling, Julep, and Lotus behind. I could leapfrog to the head of the line, but it may not be a wise decision. Royal didn't say so, but I'm sure he's timing us in here, and I don't want to waste any more time. "Clarity, you are at the head of the line, so you lead."

We move purposely through the dark for what seems like an hour without finding the exit to the maze. As a group, we walk along the length of the rope, which is strung across the room, stretched tight, with a number of turns. There is no way to mark each turn, so I have no way of counting how many there are.

"Let's turn around and go in the other direction," I say, turning toward Starling.

My team responds in the affirmative, and we shuffle back along the rope in the direction whence we came. There aren't any clues along the cord as to where the exit is located.

"Maybe we should try ducking under the rope and exploring the other side," Starling suggests.

"Let's do it," I say. I duck and move under the rope, standing on the other side.

We circumvent the maze again, arms outstretched, but find nothing but bare walls.

"Anyone got any more ideas?" I ask, frustration edging my voice.

"Nothing worth trying," Julep drawls.

"We could use some help." Haru's high voice splits the dark, but there is no response.

My team falls into silence.

I hold my hand up to my face and can't see it, even when it's pressed against the tip of my nose. A groan escapes me. This is taking much longer than it should. I fluff my hair with one hand, hoping the stimulation to my scalp will wring an idea free. It doesn't. I scan the room again, but still there is nothing to see but the blinking red light from the camera. "Are there any clues you can give us?" I ask, but again there is no answer.

We trudge onward, trying the same movements over and over again.

"Haru is gone." Clarity's voice is cool and even, but her words send goosebumps over my skin.

"What do you mean gone?" I ask. My heart begins to pound.

"She was between us, and she isn't now."

I wave my hand in front of me, grasping for anything resembling a 4'11" Japanese hacker with fluffy bangs and an unending supply of energy. My fingers slip through empty air, grasping nothing.

"She must have found the way out," Lotus says.

"Impossible," I say. "She wouldn't leave the maze without us."

"Maybe she didn't have a choice," Starling says. "Maybe once she found it, Mr. Darnay pulled her out."

I chew on that thought. It is entirely possible that Royal would remove a member of the team without alerting the rest of us. After all, it is always a possibility when we're in the field. "Okay, let's go over the maze again. Clearly, we missed something."

Time unspools in the dark, and each glance at my watch adds to my frustration. There are occasional mutterings from my teammates, but on the whole we're running out of things to say.

After a while, Julep speaks into the black. "Give a girl some help."

I roll my eyes. We aren't getting any help, not until this is over.

"Roll call," I say, my words flat.

"I'm here," Lotus says, right at my back. But that can't be. Julep and Starling were between us. I turn to face him. "Where is everyone?"

"I don't know."

"Hello?" I call.

No response.

Starling, Clarity, and Julep have also found the way out of the maze.

"We are missing something," Lotus says. "What is it?"

"If I knew I wouldn't be in here." I can't keep the anger from my voice. This is the most pointless, waste of time exercise I have ever participated in.

"Help us!" Lotus calls out, stomping a foot.

The room falls silent.

"Lotus? Are you there?"

He doesn't answer.

"Shit!"

My legs are heavy as I jog around the rope, but there's no one there. Lotus is gone, leaving me alone in the bunker.

I find one corner of the rope and yank on it with all my strength, but it doesn't come loose. It strikes me that this escape attempt is futile, because if one of my teammates had exited this way, I would have felt the vibration along the rope. But still I pull, taking out my anger on the rough cord imprisoning me here in the pitch black.

Nothing happens.

Again I duck under the rope and traverse its length, running my fingers along the walls I can reach, but find no new clues. I drag my feet along the ground feeling for something, anything, but there is nothing but the smooth concrete floor.

At last I come to a halt in the maze, my mind a blank. I have tried every method I can think of to escape from here. I am missing something obvious, but no matter what I do I can't come up with it. My face flames red. Everyone on my team has found the exit but me. I am supposed to be the best agent on our team, but clearly I am not. I've failed to exit a rope maze in an underground bunker in the Ivory Tower. I am not fit to be a teenage spy. Royal is right. He should replace me with Starling, or any other member of my team.

My short fingernails dig into my palm as I clench my fist, and release my other hand from the wiry rope. I lower my arms to my sides, shoulders squared. There is no escape now. "I give." My voice comes out low and coarse.

The lights in the bunker come on, blinding me. I blink my eyes rapidly to adjust.

Royal stands in the doorway of the bunker, a grimace on his face.

Darnay and the others stand against the wall, watching me. If I had run the entire maze with my arm outstretched, I might have been able to touch them.

"Were you all there the whole time?" I ask, my shoulders slumping.

"Yes," Royal says.

I spin around and scan the bunker. The rope is, indeed, fastened to hooks on poles so that it runs in a tight line around the room, crossing the space diagonally in several places It's strung about three feet from the walls. There is no exit that I can see.

My brows knit together and my lips purse as I turn to face Royal. "What the eff is this?" I spit the words at him. "There's no exit."

Royal folds his arms across his chest. "All you had to do to get out of the maze was utter the word, 'help.' Each of your teammates figured this out, but you." He stares at me, his clear blue eyes meeting my vivid green ones.

Anger boils up in my chest. I rip one of my karambits from my belt and swipe at the rope, slicing it clean through and watching it drop to the ground. "This is crap," I yell. "This is a crap exercise. Ask for help? Are you effing kidding me? I can't just ask for help in the field. Help doesn't magically appear and tap me on the shoulder. I have to rely on myself, my own judgment, and I have gotten the job done every single time." I jab my finger at his chest, trying to ignore the stab in my heart that comes when my mind brings up my one, epic failure— Vale's death. With effort, I force the thought to the back of my mind. "This exercise is worthless, and you know it."

Royal frowns but doesn't move to stop me as I tear past him down the hall.

Hot tears run down my cheeks as I run through the service tunnel, dropping my trench coat on the slick concrete, and leaping out into the bright light of day.

# Chapter 11

The service tunnel is quiet when I step inside, but for the swish of water through the pipes overhead, and the hum of the industrial lights. I stand in place, waiting for my eyes to adjust to the dimmer light in the space. After a moment, my eyes focus on the pipes above me and the minute cracks in the concrete floor. Stopping, I pick up my trench coat. It's damp. I sling it over my arm and plod along the tunnel, the sweat dripping down my back. Royal's voice comes through my earbud the moment I step into the Ivory Tower.

"Loveday, my office, now."

I take a deep breath to release the last remaining wisps of frustration—with him, with that stupid rope training exercise, with myself. My failure. Then I walk down the hallway and into the den, where Lotus is sprawled out on the couch, watching one of his stupid action movies. Clarity is curled into a chair, reading another book. They both look up as I enter, sympathy on their faces.

I move down the hall into the control room, where Haru is sitting at one of the desks, hunched over her laptop. She lifts her face to frown at me. "Sorry," she mouths.

My head tilts in response. Sorry, for what? But I don't ask. Instead, I scan the room for Starling, but he's nowhere to be seen. And I haven't seen Julep or Darnay since I got back either.

I shove my hands into my pockets to keep them from clenching in anger. I'm furious with myself. Starling's arrival got to me. I let him get in my head, and now my neck's on the chopping block.

"Loveday." Royal's voice is tight as he stands in the doorway to his office, hands in his slack pockets, mirroring me.

My mouth sets in a thin line and I march past Haru, past Royal, into his office. I plop into a chair facing the airplane wing desk.

My dad closes the door after me and crosses the small room to lean back against his desk, eyes leveled at me. "You know what I'm going to say." His shirt pulls at the shoulders as his arms fold across his chest.

I swallow, but don't respond.

Royal gazes at me, searching, probing for something. He sighs; whatever it is, he hasn't found it in my countenance. Whatever it is, maybe it's no longer there.

My only move is to grovel, just a little. "I know I sucked today. I let my anger get the best of me. It won't happen again."

He shakes his head. "No it won't, because I'm benching you for the foreseeable future. I can't have you out there when you aren't at your best. I won't willingly put your life on the line for work." He sets his jaw.

I propel myself out of my chair, my head shaking from side to side. "Dad, you can't do that. This is my team. I worked so hard to bring everyone together. Clarity, Lotus, Haru, and I, we're ready. Please don't do this."

He stands and rakes a hand through his short brown hair. The movement draws my eyes to his temples, where his hair is beginning to go gray.

I force my gaze back to his, and my dad's eyes bore into mine. "You've left me no choice. You step foot outside this place and you forget that you're supposed to rely on this team we've built. You go it alone every time. I can't have that."

A look of pleading seeps into my eyes. "I'll lean on my teammates more, I promise."

"We'll revisit your position on the team after we intercept the software. Until then, you'll work the concierge desk here at the hotel."

Frustration bubbles up in me like a vinegar and baking soda volcano spilling over everything, making a giant mess. "Concierge desk? Are you kidding me? You're banishing me from the Tower?"

"I know you. If you are anywhere around during our preparations, you will insert yourself. You can't help it. You've been doing it your whole life." My dad rubs the stubble on his cleft chin as he looks at me. "Maybe I should've kept you out of this. You would have been safer."

My eyes go to his desk, where there is a framed photograph of my parents on their wedding day. We've both lost loved ones.

I stand tall, rock solid on my feet, my trench coat still dangling from one arm. "I'm the one who chooses to go out there every day. I'm the one who chooses to put my life on the line. It's my prerogative."

"Not anymore." The steely look on his face chills me to the bone.

"So what will you do? Send the team out with Starling at

its head? Send a pup to do a wolf's job?"

His hands drop to his sides and a frustrated sigh escapes him. "There isn't room for lone wolves on this team."

"This is unbelievable. I never thought you'd choose a near stranger over your own flesh and blood." I glare at him before turning on my heel and leaving the room, huffing my way down the hall and into the den.

Clarity looks up from her book; it's *The Handmaid's Tale* today. She studies me with her round brown eyes, the question in them materializing in my mind. "Are you okay?"

I shake my head. "I need a few minutes to cool down." I cast a look toward Lotus, who is watching me too. He presses his watch screen to pause the movie he's watching.

I look toward the television, avoiding his pressing eyes. I won't show weakness in front of him, or any of my other teammates. Only Clarity sees that side of me, the side that is less hard as a diamond and more baby deer with wobbly legs. I school my features to conceal the fury I feel at being sidelined and plop down on the couch next to Lotus. "So, what are we watching?"

Lotus chuckles, gesturing toward the TV with one hand. "It's awesome. It's called *CheetahGator*. It's about a cheetah alligator hybrid that runs super fast and chomps people in half."

"That makes perfect sense."

"Right?!" He taps his watch again, and the movie plays.

Beside him, I relax every muscle in my body and sink into the couch, allowing my head to fall back against the cushion. I listen, past the sounds of the movie, the snapping and snarfing of a cheetahgator hybrid, through the stillness down the hallway. The sound of fingers clacking on a keyboard comes from the control room. It could be Haru or Royal at work, trying to track down The Chin. Probably both.

I turn to Lotus. "Where is everyone? Julep? Starling? Darnay?" This is still my team, and it's my job to know where each member is at all times.

Lotus licks his lips. "They went back over to Mo's. Didn't say why." He watches me for a crack in my controlled façade, any sign of weakness.

He won't get it, even though suspicion rises in me, curling around my heart and my mind. Why would they go back over there? Unless they already know that Royal has taken me off the team for the foreseeable future. If they are aware, they probably went over there to practice. Jockey for position. Julep and Starling are the likely leaders on the ground, after all.

My foot bounces on the floor, and I stand. I can't sit still right now. I run my fingers through my icy blonde hair. It's slick with sweat from my run. I turn to Clarity. "You almost ready to bleach my hair?"

"Just let me finish my chapter," she says, a smile on her lips. Then her eyes turn back to the book in her lap. She'll tell me about it later.

"I'll rinse off, and then I'll be ready." I trudge down the hall to the dormitory, grab my crap, and head to one of the two coed bathrooms at the end of the hall. A hot shower is exactly what I need to get my mind off the fact that in two short days, I've been replaced by a Manny Jacinto wannabe with surprisingly good tactical skills. I step into the shower stall and close the metal door that reaches from floor to ceiling and hang my clean clothes on the hooks on the wall. I turn on the hot water, strip, and step into the shower, closing the white curtain behind me. Here's hoping that Starling isn't as with it when he's in the field. As the thought crosses my mind, I know it's not remotely true. From what I've seen, Starling is easily as good a spy as I am. Maybe even better.

My newly bleached hair gleams as I check it in the mirror over Clarity's vanity. It looks so much better without the dark roots. I turn to her. "You ready?"

She nods, standing beside me. Today she's rocking an ashy blond bobbed wig with a button-up chambray tucked into a black leather pencil skirt. Maroon kitten heels adorn her feet. "What do you think?"

"You look great."

She beams at me. "Thanks, sis."

I tug down the black vest Darnay has provided as my uniform for my first day at the concierge desk, and roll my eyes into the back of my head.

"You look great too. Very professional."

"Shut up."

Clarity giggles as she steps toward me and puts her hands on my shoulders. She waits until I meet her eyes before speaking. "This is temporary."

I nod slightly, staring into her eyes. It had better be. "Let's go." I take a deep breath before opening the door and stepping out into the hallway. Aside from my sister, I haven't told anyone that Royal put me on desk duty, but the quiet pall that hung over dinner last night made it obvious that Julep and Starling already knew. As soon as Lotus and Haru get a look at me, it will be obvious that it's not business as usual.

The march down the hall into the control room is terribly short. Everyone is already there waiting for me. Haru is pounding away at her laptop. Lotus is sitting next to her, peering over her shoulder. Starling is sitting at the long table in the back of the room listening to something via wireless headphones, his head bobbing from side to side. I shoot an icy glare his way, and he stills but doesn't flinch.

Royal and Darnay are in the office. The murmurs of their voices are all I can hear through the closed door.

"Morning, you guys," Lotus greets us as he spins around in his desk chair.

Despite my cloudy disposition, a faint smile crosses my lips at Lotus's appropriation of Julep's normal greeting.

It's short lived. Lotus's eyebrows shoot up when he sees me, a reminder that today, I'm not a spy. "What are you wearing?" He moves across the room toward me, takes in the nametag on my chest and snickers. "Nice to meet you, Brittney."

It's a name I adopted a few jobs ago on a trip to Des Moines, and it wasn't my favorite of the monikers I've used. "Shut up."

"Oh come on. It's only for a few days. Then you'll be back down here with us." His casual confidence is at once reassuring and gut-wrenching. What if it takes me longer than that to convince Royal I'm field ready? Frustration and embarrassment burn behind my eyes.

Starling moves toward me. "I'm sorry. I didn't know I was brought here to—"

"Give me a break." I cut him off. "Usurper."

Starling's eyes go wide and he takes a step back.

Clarity clucks with her tongue and a tiny bit of guilt crops up in me. A miniscule amount. I sling my arms over my chest and plop down on the couch.

Haru simply watches us, taking in our conversation. "This is a different look for you. It suits you somehow."

"Yeah, I look like a regular real estate agent."

"A hot real estate agent," Starling mutters, his eyes flitting away from my face.

I move to stand, fists clenched, but Clarity pushes me back down. "Take a breath," she says. She sits beside me, daintily crossing her legs.

Darnay stomps out of the office, his jaw set and his eyes dark under his thick, almost black eyebrows.

Royal watches him go without saying anything. Then he turns to us. "As I'm sure you will have noticed, Loveday is going to be spending a few days at the hotel concierge desk. Julep will be your team leader until I see fit to change it." He nods at Julep, who gives a modest smile. "No problem."

"We'll go back over to Mo's this morning. Head into the armory and gather any gear you wish to take with you. I recommend you bring whatever weapon you prefer for combat in close quarters."

Clarity pats my thigh before standing and moving gracefully from the room. Lotus, Haru, and Julep follow.

Starling stands and tucks his earbuds into the pocket of his zip up jacket. He gives me a small smile before leaving the room.

Royal looks at me. "Your first shift at the concierge desk begins in five minutes. A girl named Summer will get you up to speed."

I stifle the urge to stick my tongue out at him and leave the room. The last thing I need is to make him think I'm immature, on top of being moody and reticent to ask for help. But riddle me this: when did my interior life become such a mess?

Summer is just as bouncy and enthusiastic as her name suggests. She practically squeals when I approach the desk. "Brittney! It's you!" she says, skipping out from behind the front desk to give me a hug. "I'm so glad you're here. We're going to have so much fun." She leans in, covering her mouth so that no one can read her lips. "Between you and me, the last person I worked with was a guy, and he was kind of gross. You know?" Her eyes sparkle as she takes my hand and leads me behind the desk. She bends down to retrieve a folder and slides it to me over the marble countertop. "This is the list. You can't let anyone see it; it's for our eyes only." She's serious as she says this. It makes me want to snicker, but I don't want to piss her off in my first five minutes, so I manage to hold it in.

"List?" I ask, opening the folder and flipping through the pages, each of which is neatly tucked into one of those clear plastic paper protectors. On each sheet is the name of a fancy restaurant or other establishment, and there are notes in bullet-points underneath: special guest discounts, number of tables we can claim for reservations per day, and the like.

"I've spent the last two years making friends with local business owners so I can provide our guests amazing discounts and experiences like these. I love seeing their faces light up when I tell them I can get them opera tickets to a sold out show. It's so fulfilling." She leans forward over the counter, her fair face nestled in her hands. "I think you're going to love it."

"Sounds great," I say, returning my attention to the list. There are some pretty cool things on this list—private jets, secret parks, haunted buildings, and soundscapes I want to visit someday.

"And you know what the best part is?" Summer asks, smiling wide.

"What?"

"I feel almost like a secret agent, working behind the scenes with the business owners to secure these deals. It's like I have the inside information, and if someone asks really nicely, I'll share it with them. You know?"

I bob my head. She has no idea how much I relate to what

she's talking about right now, and she never will.

# Chapter 12

By the time my shift at the concierge desk is over, I'm dead on my feet. One of the hotel's regular clients who was scheduled to arrive in the late afternoon requested that a bubble bath be drawn and ready when she arrived. In order to do this, Summer had me running upstairs every few minutes to check that the bath was still hot and bubbly. I've never used so much bubble bath in my life. Even now, the scent of cotton candy follows me as I slink through the hotel and into the service door that leads to the Ivory Tower.

My fingers are itching to put my earbud back in place. My ears felt huge and empty all day without them.

On my wrist, my watch vibrates.

**Royal**
**Come see me as soon as you get in.**

My stomach drops.

Once inside the den, I walk straight through to the control room where Royal is waiting. There's no sense in pussyfooting around. There are a lot of things to be said about me, but I don't beat around the bush. Well, unless it's a tactical choice. In this case, it won't help at all. "You wanted to see me?" I remain relaxed, nonchalant, that is, until I see the three tiny listening devices on the desk at Royal's side.

My dad's gaze follows mine down to the wooden surface, and he levels his serene blue eyes at me. "You didn't think I'd find them?"

I exhale in frustration. "Not on day one." I kick the carpet.

He gives a slight shake of his head. "Have you forgotten I taught you to use these?" He picks up one of the miniscule machines and holds it up toward me between his pointer and thumb before setting it back down on the desk. "Still, I was impressed you managed to plant this on Clarity without her even feeling it." One corner of his mouth turns up. "If I didn't know any better, I'd say you were a spy." Royal's eyes light as he chuckles.

This is a great sign, so I push my luck. "So, I take it you've realized that benching me was a huge mistake and now I can come back?"

His smile falls and his eyes grow serious. "No."

I throw my hands up. "Seriously?"

"I meant what I said. You need time to clear your head, get yourself back before I put you in the field again. Don't waste it trying to figure out what's going on back here. Maybe living life as a civilian for a while will do you some good. You might find that you enjoy it."

I clench my teeth. "I can't believe this. Life as a civilian? Do you hear yourself? I'm the best teenage spy in the world."

Royal's eyes grow hard, his mouth grim. "No, you aren't, and you won't be until you deal with your issues."

I recoil so fast he may as well have slapped me. He never speaks that harshly to anyone, least of all me. The glare I shoot his way conveys my distaste, and then I storm out of the room, eyes still blazing.

Lotus begins sniffing the air as I step into the den, laughing gleefully. He comes toward me, rubbing his hands together. He leans in and gives an exaggerated sniff of my scent. "What did they have you do? Rob a candy store?"

"Shut up," I say, shoving him away from me with both hands. I want to whale on him, but none of this is his fault. "It wasn't that bad."

"Yeah?" He nods. "Good. Good."

Maybe I can even use his sympathy for my situation to my advantage. I sidle closer to him, hoping the sugary smell that clings to me will put him in a giving mood. "So tell me, what were you guys up to all day?"

"Nope," Clarity says from behind me.

I jump at her voice and spin to face my sister.

"Can't tell," she says. "Sorry."

"Why not?" I whine, giving her a puppy dog face. "You have to tell me."

She shakes her head. "Dad made us promise not to tell. He doesn't want you sticking your nose in." She reaches out and boops the tip of my nose. "Hungry?"

I let out an exaggerated sigh to show my protest at Royal's communication ban, but my stomach grumbles, giving me away. Indistinct chatter—Haru's—wafts upstairs from the kitchen. The sound draws me forward with the promise of warmth, comfort, and a seat I don't have to get out of for an hour or more. Sitting down sounds amazing right now.

Clarity laughs. "I'll take that as a yes." She drapes an arm over my shoulders. "Come on. Starling offered to cook tonight."

My body tenses and I shrug off my sister's hand. "No thanks."

She looks down at me, frowning in disapproval, but doesn't say anything.

"Your loss," Lotus says as he leans down the stairs toward the kitchen. "Something smells amazing down there. Mmm, garlic." He trots down the stairs away from us.

Clarity moves around me and takes the first step. She pauses, turning to study me. "Are you sure you won't come?"

I shake my head. "I'll grab something from upstairs."

She bites her lip. "You can't shut him out forever." And then she's gone.

Little does she know, that's exactly what I plan to do. But first, I need to find out what they're doing in training, and I know just who I can convince to tell me. I almost give in to the desire to give an evil laugh, tapping my fingers together. Almost.

But instead, I head toward the dormitory to change clothes. After that, all I have to do is wait.

Haru practically jumps out of her skin when she walks into her room to find me sitting cross-legged on her futon, surrounded by pillows plastered with pictures of an anime couple with a tall girl and a significantly shorter guy.

"Loveday, hi!" she chirps, bouncing over the bright yellow, fuzzy rug and plopping down next to me on the futon. She wraps her arms around me and gives me a big hug. "I missed you today. It wasn't as much fun without your deadpan one-liners."

"Thanks," I say, patting her back.

She sits back and grins at me. "Guess what?"

"What?" I suppress a smirk. Maybe I won't even have to ask her. Maybe she'll spill on her own. Right now, her newness is an advantage. For me at least.

"I got to," she trails off, her eyebrows pushing together. "I'm not supposed to tell you about today, am I?" Her voice is quieter now, more uncertain.

"No, you're not," I say, shaking my head, mouth flat. Never mind. I'll have to find out another way.

"Oh my goodness. You won't tell Royal about this, will you? I don't want to get in trouble. I'm having so much fun with you all. It's so much better than being stuck upstairs in my hotel room with Ms. Truly." She says all of this at a rapid pace, cheeks flushed.

"What's there to tell? You didn't say anything."

Haru throws her arms around me again. "Thank you, thank you, thank you."

I pick up one of the pillows and study the couple hugging on its face. "Who are they?"

"Oh! You'd love them. They're friends and she's way taller than him, which he hates. Of course they fall in love and kiss under some fireworks on her birthday and it's so romantic." She sighs, having pushed this entire speech out without taking a breath.

"Sounds adorable," I say, straight-faced.

"Oh you! How come you're so serious all the time?" She hops up and crosses to her desk, opening a drawer and digging around, looking for something. Once she finds it, she spins around and holds it out to me. "Want a peach-flavored cookie stick?"

"Loveday."

I lower my book to see my sister's big brown eyes peering up at me from where she stands beside my lofted bed.

"What?" I put a bookmark in my book and close it, setting it in my lap.

She comes around to the side of the bed and climbs the ladder to sit beside me, folding her legs to one side. "I've been thinking." She pauses, twiddling her fingers. "About that program Vale installed on Dad's computer."

My head bobs. "I never got a notification or anything."

Clarity gives me a tight smile. "Do you think we could ask Haru to see if it's still running?"

"Sure." We climb down from my bed and pad across the hall to Haru's room, where she's lying in the bright yellow beanbag in the middle of her floor, eyes trained on her laptop.

"Haru?" Clarity asks, sinking into the beanbag beside the girl.

"Shh, no talking during the fuzzy part," Haru says, batting at my sister without looking away from the laptop screen.

"What's the fuzzy part?" I ask.

Haru shoots an annoyed look at me. "The part where the couple finally kiss. So shh."

I hunker down behind her and watch the screen. An anime couple are drawing closer to each other in slow motion, with hearts floating around their heads. After an agonizing amount of time, they kiss.

Haru snaps the laptop shut and turns to us. "Okay, what's up?"

We explain it to her, and by the look on Haru's face the second Clarity mentions the program, I know it's still there. Haru's eyes are wide and sparkly, and she starts nodding vigorously. In an impressive motion, she propels herself out of the beanbag chair.

Clarity slumps to the ground before standing up herself.

I stifle a laugh as Haru creeps across the room and peeps up and down the hall before answering. "It's totally still there. I found it when Royal asked me to update his security, but I figured it was a virus and paused it." She looks from Clarity to me. "Was that, was that wrong?"

I shake my head, holding up a hand. "No."

Haru visibly relaxes, her shoulders coming down from around her ears.

I weigh how much to tell her. In the six months Haru has been around, I've come to the conclusion that we can trust her, but still, it's a hard step for me to take, telling her everything. Especially after Royal's warnings. Keeping secrets seems essential to my safety, and that of my team, somehow. But I can't say no to Clarity's pleading eyes.

"The guy who used to work with us," I say.

Haru nods, mouthing, "Vale." She looks from me to Clarity and back. Someone told her about Vale. I clench my teeth. "I know we're not supposed to talk about it, but I'm so sorry. That must have been awful."

So much for secrets. "Anyway, he installed that app for us. We need to get into Royal's personal files. Can you get that program going again?"

Haru nods, bouncing on her toes. "Yes, definitely. Thanks for asking me! I'd be thrilled to help. This is so much better than working in that hotel."

"Great. Can you let us know when it's done?"

# Chapter 13

Starling marches down the staircase into the kitchen, his nose aloft. "Is that waffles I smell?"

"Yep," Lotus says from where he stands behind the kitchen counter. "I felt like eating something tasty this morning." He almost dances as he says this. "I'm tired of scrambled eggs."

"Yes," Starling says, pumping his fist. "Where's the peanut butter?"

"Peanut butter?" Clarity asks as she alights at the foot of the stairs. "I thought Lotus was making waffles." She crosses and sits beside me at the table.

"He is," I say.

"Hmm," Clarity says as she opens her book. It's *The Hate You Give* this time.

"None of you put peanut butter on your waffles?" Starling asks, his face screwed up in perplexity.

"Nope," Lotus says. "Just strawberry syrup for me." The waffle maker behind him chirps and he turns to check the waffle that's turned golden inside its hard metal shell. "Perfect. Who's up?" He plates the waffle, spins, and sets it on the counter where the butter, maple, and strawberry syrups, and powdered sugar are out and ready.

"Ladies first," Starling says. He leans back against the fridge to make room for us to reach the toppings.

Clarity and I look at each other. "You first," she says. "I'm almost done with my chapter."

"Already?" Starling asks.

Clarity's head bobs as her eyes scan the page.

"Fast reader," I say, taking the plate Starling has pushed toward me and dressing the just-the-right-amount-of-crisp waffle with butter and maple syrup.

"So, are Royal and Mr. Darnay coming down?" Starling asks as he glances up the stairs.

"No." I fill a glass with ice cold water and reclaim my place at the table.

"Royal never eats with us and Darnay left early this morning."

Starling's mouth drops open. "He did? I mean…"

Lotus laughs. "What? You were hoping he'd train with us some more?" He pours more waffle batter into the maker, and it sizzles as he closes the lid.

"Well, yeah," Starling says as his hands fall to his sides. "I could learn a lot from him."

"He's never come here before," Clarity says over her book.

"She's right," I nod. "I'm surprised he stayed as long as he did."

Starling looks crestfallen. "Oh."

The waffle maker beeps. "Clarity, you're up." Lotus dishes the waffle and slides the plate onto the counter.

My sister starts to put her book down, but Starling stops her. "I'll fix it for you. How do you want it?"

She gives him a warm smile. "Thanks. Syrup and powdered sugar please."

Haru comes flitting down the stairs as Starling is setting the plate in front of my sister. "Yum waffles! And you have peanut butter too!"

"Now, this girl's got taste," Starling says, holding out his hand to her for a high five, and she happily complies.

"Absolutely." She's still wearing what I'm pretty sure are pajamas with anime figures all over them. She catches me staring and grins. "Aren't these the best? I just got them from Ebay."

"The bestest." I bus my plate and turn to my teammates. "Don't have too much fun without me."

"Have fun doing customer service," Haru chimes in return.

"Yeah, loads."


"I've got a fun one for you today," Summer says with a grin as I approach the concierge desk. It was jarring putting on the same wig a second day in a row, but I shrugged off the unsettling feeling in the mirror, let Clarity give me a kiss on the cheek, and skulked past the control room to the exit. Unsurprisingly, Royal watched me leave to make sure I didn't overhear anything I shouldn't.

I ease around the concierge desk to face Summer, and rest one elbow on the counter and lean against it. "My kind of fun, or your kind?"

Summer crinkles her nose. "Is it so different? I thought replacing all of the photos in room 413 with photos of the cast from *Black Panther 3* was pretty fun." She stares me down, a toothy smile on her face.

"Okay, it wasn't bad." It really wasn't, mostly because the entire cast is so incredibly good-looking. I stand up straight as a group of guests bustles into the hotel, followed by an entourage of porters pushing luggage carts packed with suitcases and bags. "What's going on today?"

The car service drops me right under the Friendship Arch on the edge of Chinatown, and I make my way down the quiet streets of Chinatown. It's only 09:00, but the smells of food wafting down the street get my stomach growling. I pass a large window that's papered with giant images of dim sum, and I stop to peer inside. It's not open yet or I would definitely grab a bite to go. I could definitely eat some shrimp dumplings or sausage rolls right now.

I shake off the urge to stuff myself with a bunch of fried food and continue on down the street until I see the shop Summer told me about: it's an unassuming, olive green building tucked in between a gift shop/emporium and a huge Indian restaurant. The painted sign that hangs over the door reads, Chinese Herbs Now. I open the door and a bell chimes overhead as I step inside, letting it swing closed behind me.

A very tiny Chinese man comes out of the back room, his large, periwinkle blue sweater billowing over his jeans in a way that says it was made for a much taller guy. He takes one look at me in my hotel uniform, and grins. "How can I help you today?" he asks, moving around the corner to stand a couple feet away, looking up at me. Now, I haven't met very many people who made me feel tall, but this guy does. He has to be about 4'10", which means I'm a whole four inches taller, and it's awesome.

"I need something for the flu. Horsetail tea?"

"Right away!" He goes into the back room and speaks to

someone in Chinese. I can't make out any of it. I'd kill to have Vale with me now. He knew enough Chinese to get around. A sigh escapes me.

The proprietor emerges from the back. "It'll be ready in five minutes, but first…" He bobs his head and steps toward me, putting a hand on my elbow and spinning me so I'm facing the window. "Have a seat."

I look behind me and, sure enough, there's a low wooden stool there. I have no idea where it came from. "Why?" I ask. "Oh, the tea isn't for me."

The man ignores this and pats my arm, gesturing to the stool. "Please, sit."

"Fine." I lower myself onto the stool and wait.

The man lowers himself into a pretty impressive squat. "Stick out your tongue."

"What? No way." I shake my head.

"So stubborn," he says, clucking his tongue.

"I am not," I say. And to prove it, I stick out my tongue.

The man studies it for a long time, making small humming noises to himself as if seeing something serious.

Meanwhile, I'm hoping that the tooth brushing I did this morning is holding and my breath doesn't stink. On the other hand, he is the one who asked me to stick out my tongue, so why should I care? I'm contemplating exhaling on him when a woman walks past the window, her long brunette hair caught on the breeze. She glances into the shop window but keeps moving. My blood chills. I pop off the stool and run out of the shop, my heart in my throat, ignoring the protests of the proprietor.

The sidewalk is empty. My eyes dart back and forth scanning the street for any signs of her, and then I take off running, looking in the windows of the businesses lining the street as I pass. I dart around the corner, but she's nowhere to be seen. The woman is a ghost, an invention of my frustrated, grieving mind. I stomp a foot on the sidewalk, angry at myself for chasing something that wasn't real, and return to the herb shop.

"You're back," the man says as I enter. "Your tea is ready." He hands me a small, paper packet, and I can just see the tea leaves through the parchment. "Also, take three of these pills, twice a day until you're well." He hands me a small pill bottle of bright green capsules. "And no eating any meat until these are gone."

The Tower is silent when I get back. I walk the length of it, scanning each room, but Haru isn't even here clacking away on her laptop. I check the time on my watch. Since it's Tuesday, she's probably upstairs with Ms. Truly, our tutor. True to his word, Royal makes Haru see the tutor Tuesdays and Thursdays to keep up her education, just like he promised her mom.

A twinge of jealousy hits me at the thought. I loved Ms. Truly. She was the only teacher Clarity and I ever had. At her insistence we learned everything from the ABCs to calculus and the machinations behind governments the world over. There was even a time I'd thought Truly and my dad might be... but it never happened. I haven't seen Truly since Clarity and I graduated from high school, just after we both turned sixteen.

The delicious scent of slow cooked beef interrupts my thoughts, drawing me downstairs to the kitchen. A grin settles over my face when I see the slow cooker. Lotus must have thrown the beef and juice into the pot after I left this morning. He's really stepped up his cooking game since... well, over the last six months. I grab a fork from the silverware drawer and carefully open the lid so the hot condensation doesn't drip all over the counter. This way, Lotus won't notice if I sample it before dinner. The hot morsel is tangy sweet on my tongue as I walk back to the dormitory to change into my regular clothes.

A nap sounds amazing, so I flip the overhead light off and climb the ladder to my lofted bed, flop down on my navy blue comforter, and close my eyes. The only light in the room is the glow from the dimmed lights around Clarity's vanity. She's forgotten to turn them all the way off again.

My watch beeps and I study its face. The team is coming into the Tower through the service entrance in the parking garage. Royal and Julep come in first, followed by Clarity, Lotus, and Starling. I slide off the edge of my bed and land on my feet, meeting my teammates in the den.

"What were you all up to today?" I ask, hands slung in my trench coat pockets.

Royal smiles and gives a slight shake of his head. He brushes past me toward the armory.

"You don't give up, do you?" Julep asks, smiling wide.

"No, she doesn't," Clarity says at the same time that I say, "Nope."

Lotus pats my shoulder as he and Starling follow Royal down the hall. Starling glances back at me, but says nothing.

Julep draws near to me and leans in. "Keep pushing," she whispers. Her breath tickles the hairs at the base of my neck. "You'll get back out there."

My eyebrows raise. "Has he said something to you?"

She smiles coyly. "It's just a feeling I have." She moves off toward the armory, no doubt to divest herself of the cache of weapons she's got stowed about her person.

"Thanks," I call after her.

Clarity slings her arm around my shoulders and leans her head against mine. "She's right. Keep at it and Dad will let you back on the team at some point. Walk me to the armory?"

"All right."

We pass the rest of the team in the hall. Royal ducks into his office, and the guys make for the den. "You ready for Italian beef sandwiches?" Lotus calls over his shoulder at me.

"I was ready a half hour ago," I yell back.

Lotus laughs. "How was it?"

"I only had a bite. It wasn't enough."

He crows as he rounds the corner away from us.

I catch Clarity's eye. "It really was amazing."

She ruffles my hair and unlocks her safe, stowing a couple firearms and extra ammo inside.

I smirk at the state of it. Her safe is way less organized than mine. Royal would probably have a conniption if he got a look in there. It's a good thing he doesn't do gun safe inspections anymore. He stopped those when we were around fourteen, once he'd made damn sure we knew how to properly store our weapons so that no one got shot accidentally. Well, after that one time. It took twenty minutes for the tranquilizer dart I'd shot in his foot to wear off, and then he'd yelled. Loud. The memory brings a smile to my face.

"Hey," Clarity whispers, drawing my attention back to her.

"Hey."

"How was it at the concierge desk today?" She gestures toward the hallway and I nod in assent.

"Fine. Boring." I shuffle down the hall behind Clarity, marveling at her grace. I have no idea how she moves like a ballerina even though she's never had lessons, but she does. "How was training?"

My sister looks over her shoulder at me. "You know I can't tell you."

We pass through the den, where Lotus and Starling are

hunched over game controllers and staring at the flat screen TV tucked into one corner. Julep is sitting in a plush chair to one side, knitting a cable sweater. "Looks great, J," I say as Clarity and I pass through to the dormitory.

Once we're in our room I shut the door behind us. "You're killing me," I say, leaning against the closed portal.

"I'm sorry," Clarity responds, sinking into her desk chair and getting out the latest issue of *Vogue* and a pair of scissors.

I huff. "It's not that I want to get back in the game…" I trail off as Clarity shoots a look at me, eyebrow raised.

"Okay, I do, but really I just want to make sure you're all safe, and it's killing me that I'm not there to make sure of it."

Clarity sits back in her chair and turns toward me. "I understand that." She licks her lips. "I know you aren't going to want to hear this, but you don't have to worry. We're doing well as a team. And Starling is a great field agent."

I roll my eyes. "You're right; I don't want to hear about him." I cross to my desk and plop into my desk chair, pulling open my drawers and looking for something, anything, to occupy my mind.

"Come on, Sis," Clarity says behind me. "You've got to learn to trust him sometime."

"No I don't. Especially when I haven't seen him in training. For all I know, he could be Mr. Bean."

My sister laughs out loud at this. "He's not." She quiets. "I probably shouldn't say this, but we were training at Fashion Center today, and he picked Lotus's pocket three times."

I snort. "Lotus must be off his game."

"No, he's not. Starling is really good. His brush passes are quick and effective, and he's great at finding gaps in surveillance. He's a great spy."

So am I, sis. Or, more accurately, I used to be.

# Chapter 14

After two weeks at the concierge desk, it feels like my spy skills are fleeing my brain, draining out of my ears as I sleep, kind of like the information you cram before a test but forget about immediately after. But Royal seems to be softening his stance regarding my return to the team. Yesterday he mentioned that someone needs to visit our CIA dead drop spot in the next few days, and hinted that he might let me do it. I'm walking past the waterfall in the hotel atrium when my watch vibrates. The message brings a grin to my face. I run the rest of the way down to the Ivory Tower, exhilaration coursing through me. I'm back, baby.

"What do you need me to do?" I ask as I burst into his office. "Visit the dead drop? Bump and grab? Brush past? I'm ready."

Royal purses his lips. His scrutinizes me for a minute, and I remain still to hide the coil of unease unfolding in me.

"I'm not reinstating you," Royal says as he leans forward in his chair, forearms resting on his desk. "You need time."

"What? No I don't." I lean forward over his desk, hovering above him. "I'm fine."

Royal exhales. "Just take Lotus out to the airfield, will you? That's all I'm asking right now. He needs the practice. And I was hoping this would help you not feel so..." His voice trails off as he eyes me. "Useless."

The word is like a stone in the pit of my stomach. It ricochets through my mind, echoing the clamor that's been sounding since Starling arrived. So that's it; Royal does think I'm replaceable. Pricks rise behind my eyes, but I don't let them win. To cry is to show weakness, and I won't do that in front of Royal, not when I'm already completely exposed. "Okay, I'll take him."

"Try to enjoy it." He pleads with his eyes, willing me not to hate him.

"Will do." I turn and leave the office before I say anything that pushes me over the edge. I bite my tongue to hold the tears back as I advance toward the dormitory to give Lotus the news. But the voices I hear under the current of music blasting from his room stop me. He's not alone in there.

"Are you dense?" Julep whisper-shouts. "You saw what it's done to Loveday."

"Well, I just won't die, then you won't have to miss me." The flirt flows through his words.

I creep closer to Lotus's room, being careful not to make any noise. I have to hear this.

Julep laughs, but it sounds muffled, like she's covering her mouth with her hands.

"Just give me a chance. You won't regret it."

Julep's voice is full of resignation. "It's too dangerous. It'll compromise both of us. We can't do that to the rest of the team."

I'm stunned. How long has this been going on? Whatever it is, they are obviously much more successful at hiding it than

Vale and I were. My head feels weighed down, so I allow it to drop forward.

"We'll be fine. I don't want to miss out on this." Lotus again, his voice as smooth and earnest as I've ever heard it.

It's quiet for a minute before Julep speaks again. "I'll think about it."

I spirit away to my room before anyone can see me. My heart beats in the pit of my stomach as I close the door. I'll tell Lotus after dinner, right before it's time to go. From the sound of it, he'll need some time to unwind after the conversation he just had with Julep.

The timer on the oven reads three minutes when I step down the final stair into the kitchen. "It smells so good," I say, trotting over to the counter, where Clarity is peering into the oven.

"It's bubbling nicely," she says as she straightens. "Want to help me get plates and silverware?"

"Consider it done." I dart around the kitchen, retrieving plates and glasses from the upper cabinets and silverware from one of the drawers.

"Ice those, will you?" Clarity asks, pointing at the glasses set out on the counter.

"Sure."

"I can do that," Starling says as he jogs over from the bottom of the stairs. His arm brushes mine as he leans past me toward the glasses, and warmth creeps up my arm. I recoil, cursing my skin for reacting that way to my rival, and shove my arms into my trench coat to hide the goosebumps along my fair skin.

Clarity furrows her eyebrows at me, but shakes her head and refocuses on her lasagna.

Laughter precedes Lotus and Julep down the stairs, and he bumps his shoulder against hers. I'm not sure if it was intentional.

A sly smile crosses Julep's face before she lifts her face toward us. "Oh. Can I help with anything?" She bustles over to the counter and scoops up the silverware, moving to set it out on the table.

My eyes cut to Lotus, who scratches at his neck as he grabs two of the glasses Starling has filled and sets them on the table. "Sparkling cider, huh? Fancy."

"Isn't it?" Clarity says with a smile. "A client sent it to Royal, and he said we could drink it."

"He's letting us drink alcohol?" Starling asks, a look of confusion on his face.

"Ha, no," Lotus says with a chuckle. "It's just fizzy apple juice."

"Oh." Starling carries the remaining glasses to the table.

The oven beeps, and Clarity opens it and pulls out the lasagna. It's a huge pan full of tangy tomato, soft noodles, and cheese. All the cheese. "Come and get it," she says as she sets it on a couple hot pads on the concrete countertop.

"Where's Haru?" I ask, moving across the kitchen to glance up the stairs.

A flurry of footsteps sounds above me, and Haru tears around the corner and down the stairs. "I'm sorry I'm late," she calls as she flies off the bottom step, panting. "I was in the control room with Royal. He just got some intel on where the CIA thinks The Chin is right now. They think he's in…" Her eyes land on me, and her mouth clamps shut. "Sorry, I thought you were still upstairs."

I suppress the urge to glower, and instead merely say, "Nope."

"Let's eat, shall we?" Clarity asks, carrying two full plates of food over to the table.

Once we're done eating, I push away my plate, which I've scraped clean of any traces of lasagna, and lean back in my chair. "Clarity, that was the best lasagna you have ever made."

It's been pretty quiet during our meal, partly because of Haru's entrance and partly because the meal was delicious. All of my teammates are sitting around the trestle table, finishing up their dinner.

"Thanks." Clarity looks like the cat that ate the canary as she picks up the plates from around the table and carries them to the counter.

Starling pops out of his chair. "Let me do those. You did all the cooking."

"You don't have to twist my arm," Clarity says, leaving the dishes in the sink and returning to the table to sit beside me.

"I'm going to have to do some exercise if we keep eating like this," Lotus says with a laugh, grabbing his nonexistent stomach fat and jiggling it vigorously.

Haru giggles into her hand.

"Speaking of exercises," I say, raising an eyebrow at Lotus.

"Aww, don't be mean," Lotus says, batting a hand at me.

"That's not what I have in mind," I say, pushing back from the table and standing. "Royal says you need to practice flying at night. Get your gear. Let's go."

As what I have said dawns on Lotus, a grin explodes over his face, making him look like an enthusiastic jack-o'-lantern. "Are you kidding me?"

"Nope." I shake my head, my hands resting in my trench coat pockets. "I want to leave in ten minutes."

"Yeah?" Lotus stands up, practically bouncing with excitement. "Okay. I'll be ready." He practically runs from the room to grab his gear.

"That sounds brilliant. Can I tag along?"

The eagerness in Starling's voice turns me cold. My mouth forms a straight line. "No." I don't even look at him. Instead, I climb the stairs into the den, ignoring the pall of disappointment that follows me from the kitchen. Not just Starling's, but Julep and Clarity's too.

The plane is enveloped in darkness. It's peaceful and quiet up here. I never want to go back down again. "This is amazing," I breathe, looking over at Lotus.

He's got his headphones on and is totally focused on his instruments and controls. So far, the flight has been smooth as silk. I've got to hand it to Royal. He has taught Lotus well.

"Isn't it?" He turns us a little to the left before continuing. "When I was in foster care, you know, back in —"

"Don't tell me where." From his accent and vocabulary early on, I already surmised where he's from, but I keep up the pretense. Royal would call it, "plausible deniability."

"Sorry. But you know I was in foster care."

I nod. "Yeah. I know that much."

"Well, I used to steal cars and go joyriding."

"I knew that too."

He meets my eyes, and, after studying me a moment, he must decide that he's okay with what he sees there, because he continues. "I liked to see how fast I could go before I got caught. I used to pretend I was flying. It helped that it was hilly there, where I lived."

"I bet." This was his dream, flying a plane. Just like being a spy was mine. "Does it feel like how you imagined it would?"

The plane floats through the inky black outside the window. I look down at the lights of the city below us. It's all oranges and yellows, with streaks of red and white as cars move along the streets.

"No. This is a million times better."

We fall quiet again, enjoying the stillness of the air in the tiny plane. My thoughts drift to the specter that has been haunting me both in my dreams and during my waking hours. I never saw her before Vale died, but now she is everywhere. My mom. I can't seem to shake her. It's as if seeing Vale die in my arms brought the reality of my mom's death crashing in on me in a way that I never felt before. I wish I could ring out all of my emotions and tuck them away for a better time and place, but I can't. "Lotus?"

He glances over at me, a quizzical look on his face. "Yeah?"

"You have to help me train for this mission. I have to be ready. Working the concierge desk is driving me nuts. I'm starting to see things that aren't there." I laugh to hide the truth of my words, and Lotus chuckles along with me.

I go still beside him, and he looks over at me. "You're not kidding, are you?"

I lick my lips. "No."

He eyes me for a second before turning his attention forward again, and lets out a sigh. "Yeah, okay. I'll help you."

"Thanks." I wonder what Lotus would think if he knew that I was seeing glimpses of my mom, flickers that feel completely real. I wonder what Clarity and Royal would think. What Haru would think. And even Starling. And I realize in that instant: they can't know. They can't ever know.

# Chapter 15

We're sitting around the table eating breakfast pizza, my creation, when Lotus lifts his eyes to mine. "I need to hit the mall today, find a new hoodie. You in?" He takes a swig of his orange juice and closes his eyes, as if the question he's asking me is no big deal.

Immediately I catch his meaning. "Definitely."

Clarity leans forward in her chair, eyeing Lotus. "Didn't you buy a new hoodie last week?"

"That one was black. I need a blue one." Without missing a beat, he takes a bite of the flaky, puff pastry pizza.

"Can I come?" Haru asks. "I need to pick up a new solid state drive for my laptop. And maybe a backup hard drive. Oh, and a new laptop skin."

Lotus laughs. "Sure. The more the merrier."

I shoot him a look. That's not exactly true. I'm not sure I could convince Clarity to keep her mouth shut if she finds out what we're up to.

"I'll come too," my sister says. "I need some new makeup."

Apparently, I'm going to find out how persuasive I really

am. If Julep were here, it would be even trickier, but she's off doing a small job for Royal.

"Sounds awesome," Starling says. "When are we leaving?" From his solid stance, I can see that he won't take "no" for an answer this time.

"Why are you wearing a wig?" Clarity asks as she stands in the doorway of our bedroom, hands on her hips.

"I just felt like a change," I say as I bend down to get a view of myself in the mirror over her vanity. I make sure the long, caramel colored wig is on straight, and stand.

"Right," Clarity says slowly. She's not buying it. She probably already knows why we're really going shopping, and unlike Lotus, she refused to help me against Royal's wishes. I'm still annoyed at her. What's a sister for, if not helping you break a few rules without getting caught?

"I'm going to get a snack for later," I say, brushing past her.

"I'll come too. A snack sounds good." She follows me down the hall to the kitchen.

I manage to send a message to Lotus while Clarity is rummaging around in the pantry for a protein bar and an individual serving size packet of dried seaweed. He'll have to get our supplies since Clarity's acting clingy like baby opossums on their mom's back.

I put a string cheese in the deep pocket of my trench coat and lean back against the counter, waiting for Clarity to emerge from our food storage.

"You ready?" I say when she straightens.

"Yes," she says. "What do you need at the mall again?"

"Did you get them?" I whisper to Lotus as we walk toward Royal's van. Clarity, Haru, and Starling trail behind. Clarity, at least, is probably watching us.

Lotus pats his jeans pocket in response.

I'd have gotten the earbuds myself, but Clarity wouldn't leave me alone after breakfast.

It's Saturday, but even at 09:00 the mall is already crawling with people. It'll make training much more complicated, but at least it'll be easier to lose our hangers-on in the crowd. We pass through the tall glass doors and I step to the side so people can pass. "We'll meet back here in two hours, okay? Good."

I grab Lotus by the crook of the arm and charge off into the crowd without waiting for a response. A glance over my shoulder reveals Haru chattering away with Starling, who looks disappointed at our abrupt departure, a frown on his face and shoulders slumped. Clarity stands apart, arms crossed, watching us as we push further into the crowd.

"We'll start with a brush pass," Lotus says once we're confident we've lost our teammates. We're standing near the mouth of the food court. He points upward. "But we have to avoid the cameras. Find a blind spot and I'll meet you there."

This shouldn't be hard. I've played this game at malls plenty of times. But this isn't our usual mall, and there are way more cameras here than I'm used to. "Must be all the high end stores," I whisper.

"What?" Lotus asks. "I didn't catch that."

"Nothing," I say, biting my lip as I scan for a blind spot. "Found one. Over there."

"Okay, now comes the tricky part." Lotus rubs his hands together.

"Tricky part?"

He nods. "Oh yeah."

I can't believe I'm doing this: stealing three fries from an unsuspecting diner in the middle of the food court. And it has to be three. I walk along the edge of the food court, pretending to scan the food vendors, but really I'm looking for someone who isn't paying attention to their food.

Finally! I stroll toward a table of three teenage boys, probably a year or two younger than me, each of whom is zoned out on their phone. There's an untouched container of fries dangerously close to the edge of the table, and it'll work perfectly for my purposes.

The container of fries flops off the table as I brush past, pocketing three. Then I spin around and bend down, shoveling the remaining fries back into the container. "I'm so sorry," I say without looking up at the boys who are now staring down at me. "I can't believe I did that." Once all the fries are back in the container, I stand up and meet their eyes with my best doe eyed look on. "I'm so sorry," I say again, training my gaze on the boy closest to me. "Can I buy you some fries as an apology?" I'm counting on him saying no, because I've only got twenty seconds to get to the blind spot.

He gets one look at me and jumps out of his chair.

Crap. This is going to cost me time I don't have. I scan the food court for Lotus and find him snickering into his hand fifty yards away, so he's no help.

Fry boy shakes his head. "No, don't worry about it. I wasn't even eating those." He glances at his friends, who motion him onward. He turns back to me. "So, um, can I buy *you* some fries?" He blushes as he smiles at me, his expression a little embarrassed but hopeful.

I giggle. "Oh no, I couldn't let you do that! It's my fault you lost your fries after all. I insist you let me buy you some." I'm counting on him not wanting to let me do that in front of his friends.

"No, that's okay. It's no big deal."

"Thanks so much," I chirp over my shoulder as I hustle toward the blind spot, but freeze in the middle of the walkway. There's a mom standing in the exact spot I'm aiming for, trying to calm her crying toddler. There's not enough room for me to wedge myself into position between her and the ficus tree that marks the edge of the security camera's field of view, and I've only got five seconds left.

My pulse quickens as I look skyward, scanning the areas covered by security cameras. I follow their direction and see Starling standing across the way, beckoning me toward him. He's standing in another spot shielded from the cameras.

Screw it. I can't blow this exercise, so I stalk toward Starling, grumbling about how he's somehow gotten involved in my training with Lotus. He must have followed us and been watching to figure out what we were doing. I shimmy behind the pillar and stop beside Starling just as my watch beeps. Time is up and I haven't successfully completed the brush pass. The cameras shift and the blind spot vanishes.

I stomp my foot, cursing under my breath. My gaze travels up to Starling, who shrugs, an easy smile on his face. "Next time."

The casual way he says it makes my insides burn with anger, which is good because otherwise I'd be all too aware that he and I are hiding alone in a secluded alcove behind a large stone pillar. I shoot a glare at him, both for the way my body reacts to his nearness, and because of his spot on my team. He can afford to be casual about training because he's currently on the team, whereas I'm exiled to the concierge desk. It's basically espionage Siberia. I open my mouth to retort when Starling's eyes lift and focus on something over my shoulder.

"It wouldn't kill you to ask for help," Clarity says from behind me. "I could have gotten you the fries without having to stop to flirt." A corner of her mouth curls upward.

I'm scowling now. "Maybe." Asking for help might not be the death of me, but what about the poor soul who answers when I call?

# Chapter 16

This is not what I had in mind when Royal finally asked me to visit the dead drop this evening. My hands grip the steering wheel as I look over at Starling, who's stretched out in the passenger seat next to me. The urge to roll my eyes is strong, and I give it full reign. Apparently I'm doing a bang up job of disguising my vehement hatred at the notion that Starling has taken my spot on my team, because Royal's sent us on a stupid errand. Really, I did not need help for this. It's a simple dead drop. All I have to do is retrieve a thumb drive from under a garbage can lid. And yet I'm driving Royal's car away from the hotel with Starling as my only passenger. The old man wouldn't even let Clarity come with us as a buffer.

Stubbornness clamps my mouth shut as I drive. I might as well have a strip of duct tape over my lips, because nothing is going to make me talk to the tall, sinewy, annoying man-child with the piercing eyes who's sitting in the seat beside me.

It's late in the evening, so traffic is starting to thin out, but not enough to make us conspicuous on the street.

We're almost there.

"Shouldn't we do a cover stop or something?" Starling breaks the silence hesitantly, like he's afraid I'll smack him if he speaks.

"Why do you think I got a shopping list from Clarity?" I shoot an arched eyebrow in his direction.

"I thought as much," he says, glancing at me before returning his focus to the street in front of us. "There's a parking space right up there." He points to an open spot on the left. It'll be tight, but I can make it.

Once the street clears, I pull a U-turn, slide the car into reverse, and parallel park with ease. Satisfaction bubbles up in me. I've always been good at parallel parking. Even Lotus had to applaud the first time he saw me do it. I have to admit, it made me feel pretty good.

"Smooth," Starling says as we unbuckle, climb out of the car, and step up to the sidewalk.

I grunt in his direction. I'd rather ignore him completely, but Royal didn't raise Clarity and me to be rude. When someone speaks to me, I'm compelled to respond in some way. A grunt is about the least I can do without guilt creeping in. I take the list Clarity's given me out of the pocket of my coat and tear it in half. "You take the produce and meats and I'll take everything else."

Starling takes the ripped paper from my hand and reads it. "She organizes her grocery list by category?"

I laugh. "No."

"Then how?" He looks back down at the list and up at me. "You. You did this."

I shrug.

A small smile creeps over Starling's face. "My aunt does this." He laughs. "She says it saves time."

"She's right." I push into the store, and Starling reaches over me to hold the door.

"Thanks," I say, since grunting this time would definitely

be rude. Besides, he's being so nice to me that I'm starting to feel like crap for avoiding him the past couple weeks. He looks down at me with those dumb, soft brown eyes and I change my mind. "I'll meet you in front of the self-check kiosks in fifteen minutes," I say in a gruff voice before scooping up a hand basket and stalking off down the aisle. I'm not giving him a chance to answer.

I'm almost done shopping, and the basket is getting pretty heavy in the crook of my arm, when movement in my peripheral vision catches my eye. It's her again. My arms go slack and my shopping basket slips down toward my wrist. I grab the handle just before it slips past my fingers and set it on the squeaky clean linoleum before racing down the aisle after her. I saw my mom. I did. I take the corner, my feet slipping as my tennis shoes struggle to grip the slick linoleum floor, and sprint across the front of the store, looking down each aisle in turn.

She's not there. She's nowhere to be found.

Frustration builds in me as I walk the length of the store again, looking down every aisle and every checkout line. She's not there.

There's a light tug on the arm of my coat. "You ready?" Starling asks.

My face must be paler than normal when I turn toward him, because his black eyebrows shoot up and he steps toward me. "Are you okay?"

I nod. "Yeah, let's go." But I'm not fine. My hands tremble as we scan our items, and they don't stop until I'm outside on the curb, staring at our car.

"Do you want me to drive?" Starling asks as he sidles up beside me.

"No, I'm fine," I say, propelling myself around the car and

into the driver seat.

Starling slides into the passenger seat, a look of unease on his face.

"You okay?"

"Yes, I'm fine," he responds, but the exhale he tries to suppress doesn't fool me. Still, I don't push it.

Instead, I maneuver our car out into the flow of traffic and drive toward the location we're using for the dead drop tonight.

I parallel park again, but this time it's not the best. It's a good thing we'll be parked here for less than a minute, because I'm way too far from the curb. I look over at Starling, who's studiously avoiding looking at me.

"Let's see what you've got," I say, gesturing toward the electric car charging station that's sitting on the curb next to our parking spot. They've become a ubiquitous sight around the city over the past decade. "The code is 717390."

Starling gives me an easy smile before sliding out of the car and walking up to the kiosk. There's no fidgeting or overt glancing around as he punches in the code and waits. Instead, he seems more at ease out on that curb than he has for the past ten minutes of our drive. To anyone passing by, he's just a teenage boy preparing to plug in his electric car.

I scan the street. There are shoppers on the sidewalk, most of whom are carrying canvas bags loaded down with sundry items. No one is watching Starling, who glances up and around casually before returning his attention to the kiosk. A slatted panel below the charging cable opens. Starling pockets the item, closes the panel, and gets back in the car.

I steer us away from the curb and back toward the hotel, my fingers wrapped around the steering wheel at ten and two. It's a push, but I manage to speak. "That was pretty smooth back there."

"Yeah?" Starling asks as his face lights up.

"Yeah. Go ahead and send Royal a message that we've made the pick-up."

"Yes, ma'am."

I raise an eyebrow. "Really?"

He chuckles as he types into his watch.

"What'd you write?" I ask. He probably used one of those stupid phrases like, "The phoenix is rising," or some nonsense like that.

"I told him the store had the crackers he asked for."

A begrudging smile crosses my face. It turns out, Starling's a good spy, damn it.

When we get back to the Tower, Clarity, Lotus, and Julep are cozy in the den, snuggled in blankets and roaring with laughter. One glance at the TV explains the mirth. "Spy movie mock fest?" I ask, plopping down in the plush chair next to Clarity's. Lotus and Julep, I notice, are sitting pretty close on the couch, although each of them has their own blanket. I feign an arm stretch and crane my neck, but I can't see their inside hands. If I had to bet I'd guess they're at least touching pinkies under there.

Starling's eyes flit to mine. He's caught their nearness as well. Without warning, he plops down next to Lotus and pulls the blanket toward himself. Sure enough, Julep's hand flies up to her lap as the blanket exposes it.

"What the hell, man?" Lotus turns to Starling and tugs the blanket back over himself, his voice full of surprise.

"I'm cold," Starling says with a sheepish expression.

With a flick at her watch, Clarity pauses the movie and turns toward the boys, eyeing them.

"Get your own," Lotus says, pulling on the blanket that's

stretched tight between him and Starling.

"There are extras in the ottoman," Clarity says, tapping it with her foot.

"No way. This one's soft," Starling says, yanking on the blanket again. "You get your own."

Lotus busts up laughing at this. "Not a chance."

"Guys!" I say, but they're not listening. I heave myself out of my chair with an eye roll, get two more blankets out of the storage ottoman at Clarity's feet and toss one to Starling.

"Now can we get back to the movie?" Julep asks, amusement in her voice.

"Children," Clarity says with a shake of her head. "We're almost to the good part."

"Where the main guy jumps down on top of a helicopter and doesn't get sliced to ribbons?" I ask. Watching spy movies and making fun of them the entire time is one of our favorite things to do when we're not training. It's hilarious how badly moviemakers get the spy trade wrong.

My sister nods as she starts the movie again.

"Excellent."

# Chapter 17

The hotel lobby is buzzing with guests talking about the summer Olympics starting next week in St. Petersburg. Apparently the athletes have started to arrive to much nicer accommodations than they had in Sochi, meaning they have electricity and clean water this time. The only reason I know about it is that the terrible accommodations the Russians provided last time they hosted have been all over the news. It's pretty funny actually, imagining journalists in Sochi to cover the Olympics without access to basic stuff like Internet and working toilets.

I don't care about that so much, but I am really looking forward to the synchronized diving and swimming competitions. The amount of work they must put in to matching the movements of their partners is astounding to me. And I've already talked Clarity into staying up all night to watch it with me, because they aren't important enough events to air during the day. Which is pretty stupid.

I tap my fingers on the concierge desk. There isn't much to do with Summer out of the office today meeting with one of her contacts. Yes, Summer has contacts. I found it hard to believe at first, that a concierge must have friends who work at local businesses, but it's true. And Summer is actually really good at being a concierge.

"Hey," Clarity smiles at me as she advances toward the concierge desk wearing her usual cream colored button-down blouse and olive green slacks.

"No training today?"

"Royal gave us a break for Lotus's birthday. And he's milking it. He wants us to go to some new go-cart racing place later."

"Sounds fun," I say as Clarity comes around the desk and leans forward on her forearms, her eyes scanning the lobby. "What are you doing? People watching?"

"Pretty much. I don't have anywhere else to be." Clarity meets my eyes and gives me a small smile. Then she holds out a hand and waves forward someone I didn't see before. Starling. He hovers a few feet away from the concierge desk, watching us, hands in the pockets of his slim-fit jeans.

I let out a groan. "What is he doing here?" I glare at my sister.

"Don't look at me like that. I want us all to have fun tonight, together, not in separate factions."

"There are factions now? Whose side are you on?"

"Don't do that," she says, giving me a firm look. "Eventually, Dad is going to put you back on the team, and when he does you need to be on speaking terms with every single member. Including the ones you insist on treating badly."

I sigh. "Fine." I wave him forward.

He approaches the desk and puts his palms down on the smooth, deep mahogany surface. "How's it going out here?" he asks, not quite meeting my eyes. Whatever ground we'd made up during our dead drop run last night, we lost when he heard the conversation Clarity and I had just now.

I deserve this shy treatment; I've pretty much been an ass to him since he arrived.

"It's fine. There's not a lot going on right now, aside from that." I point at the headline on the tablet that's glowing on the counter to our left. Reading news articles is my chosen way to kill time while Summer is away from the hotel. She encouraged me to do it by saying that it would keep me current on the happenings in the city. "That way, we can anticipate all of our clients' needs," she'd said.

"Right, the Olympics. I've always wanted to go," Starling says, picking up the tablet and scrolling down. "I'd love to see the synchronized diving in person. I bet it's amazing."

I narrow my eyes at him. "Did my sister tell you to say that?" I turn to look at Clarity, but she's gone, disappeared back into the crowded lobby.

"Seriously, how does she do that?" Starling shakes his head in admiration and sets the tablet back down on the counter.

"Got me," I say, shrugging. A quick scan of the crowd reveals neither hide nor hair of Clarity. "She's probably back in the Tower by now."

"Look," Starling says, standing up straight and meeting my eyes. "This wasn't what I imagined when Royal invited me here. I had heard so many stories about you from Julep and I was really looking forward to working with you and getting to know you." His serious, deep brown eyes don't move from my green ones. It's an intense gaze, and I can't hold it. I look down at the tablet.

"Well, apparently that's not what Royal had planned." My voice comes across with more edge than I intended, but I don't apologize for it. The truth is that my situation is my fault, Royal's fault, and only a little bit Starling's fault. But he is the easiest to blame.

Starling sighs, frustration seeping into his voice. He pushes back from the counter and bumps into a middle-aged woman who was passing behind him. Mortified, he spins to face her. "I'm so sorry, ma'am. Are you all right?"

The woman nearly swoons at the sound of his accent. "Oh, I'm fine. Thank you." She gives him a smile before moving off across the atrium.

Starling turns back to me, and clears his throat. "That was close."

"Yeah. You were going to say something?"

His eyes snap to mine at the blunt way I speak. "Right. Um, this is the best thing that's ever happened to me, and I was thrilled when Julep told me about you guys..." He pauses, shifting on his feet. "But you clearly don't want me here. What would you have me do? Quit?"

For a second, I want to answer in the affirmative. Part of me would love it if he were gone from the Ivory Tower, because up to now he's been mostly a huge annoyance. But the rest of me recognizes that if I'm not going to be on the team whenever they go after The Chin, my teammates will need all the help they can get. From what little I have seen of Starling during training, he's the real deal. A born spy. Admitting this might kill me, but the team needs him. I need him to take care of them if I'm not going to be there. I force my eyes up to meet his. "No. I don't want you to quit."

A smile creeps up his face as he looks at me. "You don't?"

It's an effort not to look away. "Don't get too excited. I'm not making you a favorite contact on my watch or anything."

His smile widens. "Still, I'll take it." He extends his hand across the desk toward me.

I eyeball it for a moment before taking it. "Now get out of

here, will you? I'll probably have to pick all of the green M&Ms out of a bag here pretty soon."

Starling laughs outright now. "Is that what you've been doing up here? Sorting candy?"

"Something like that."

"That's kind of a waste of time for the best teenaged spy in the world." The clear admiration in his eyes makes me turn my eyes away.

"Would you tell Royal that for me?"

"I will, but he seems pretty stubborn."

My eyes find his again. "Family trait."

Starling laughs, and then heads toward the waterfall in the center of the lobby. That entrance is my favorite way into the Tower, and also one of the least practical. It'll be a challenge to get under there without being noticed by someone in this crowd. I watch him carefully until he steps under the waterfall. Sure enough, he does it without anyone noticing that there's a teenage boy playing in the water feature in the middle of the hotel atrium.

A smile creeps toward my lips as I return my focus to the people checking into and out of the hotel. Summer should be back soon with something moderately interesting and exceedingly tedious for me to do, like set the alarm to play the Olympic fanfare or something.

Even though Summer keeps me busy for my entire shift, my mind won't focus. Instead, it keeps replaying the incident in the grocery store. I'm almost positive I saw my mom, but that's impossible. When my shift is finally over, I hustle back to the Tower to find it almost empty. Where is everyone? I shrug as I walk down the hall to the dormitory. No music comes from Lotus's or Haru's room, and Clarity isn't in our room either.

My mouth purses as I shut my door and cross to my desk, sinking into the desk chair. They must still be out training.

Leaning down, I slide open the bottom drawer of my vintage desk and pull out the framed photo of my mom. I've looked at it, her face, a thousand times, but it doesn't usually cause an ache like the one in my heart today. The glimpses I've caught of her around town have made it so much harder not to think about her and all that I've missed out on since my mother died.

I fluff my hair with one hand before pushing back from the desk and standing. With careful steps, I wade across the mess that is Clarity's clothing on our floor and swipe her tablet from where she's left it on her unmade bed. It only takes one search to find what I'm looking for: the newspaper article that detailed my mom's car accident sixteen and a half years ago. Photos of the crash, stark and ugly, glow on the screen of the tablet. In them, the hood of my mom's car is crumpled like a wad of tissue paper. A metal guardrail has pierced the windshield, shattering the glass into a million tiny shards. I wince at the images. There's no way she walked away from that accident. But it's strange; why was she on the road that night? I need to know.

I set the tablet back where I found it and jog down the hall, through the den, and into the control room. The door to Royal's office is closed. I stand outside it, stretching out a hand to knock without hesitation.

"Come in," Royal says through the door.

My shoulders come down from around my ears. He can answer all of my questions.

I slide into the tiny office, closing the door behind me. "I've been thinking about Mom." I sit on the edge of the chair facing his airplane wing desk.

Royal's eyes meet mine, and then flick down to the framed photo on his desk. I know from memory that it's a photo of Royal holding me as a baby, and Mom is standing to the side, resting one hand on his arm, watching him look at me. All the same, I stand up and move around the desk so I can see it.

"This was taken a few weeks before the crash," I say as I put my fingers to the glass.

Royal clears his throat. "Yes, it was. You'd just said Daddy for the first time. I'll never forget the sound of your tiny voice calling me Da Da." In an uncharacteristic move, he puts one arm around my waist and draws me close. We remain there for a moment, looking at the photo together, our sides touching.

"Hey, Dad?" I ask as I straighten and lean against the desk, facing him. "I know we were in a car crash, and it was late at night, but it's been bothering me. Why was Mom driving me somewhere at 2300 hours? Aren't babies usually in bed by then?"

He sits back in his chair and folds his hands. "They are, yes."

"So?" I raise my shoulders, prompting him to continue.

A sigh escapes him. "I'm ashamed to admit this, but your mom and I had a pretty nasty fight. She was going to stay with her sister for a few days."

My jaw drops open. "Mom was leaving? And also, I have an aunt out there somewhere?"

"No. No." He shakes his head. "She wasn't leaving me. She needed time to cool off. We both did. And I don't know if her sister is still living. We haven't kept in touch."

"Can't you look her up or something?" I ask, incredulous. I might have a cool aunt out there who could tell me more about my mom. I'm stunned that Royal never told me about her, but then I understand why he didn't: to keep Mom's family from discovering his job. So of course my parents didn't spend a lot of time at family events, if at all.

His words niggle at my brain. "What were you fighting about?" I ask. What could have been so bad that my mom would need to step away? From all of the stories Royal has told me, they loved each other desperately. That doesn't jibe with what he's telling me now.

He shrugs. "I don't remember."

I study him for a second because this seems way too cliché to be true, but he's not showing any signs of lying. Besides, he often says that marital fighting is more about the events that lead up to the fight anyway, and not the fight itself. It must be what happened here, but I'd still love to know what they were fighting about. Too bad there's no way to find out.

# Chapter 18

The rest of my teammates come bursting through the service door into the den just as I open my book.

"There you are!" Clarity says, patting the top of my head.

"Here I am," I respond, closing my book and setting it on the arm of the chair.

Behind my sister, Lotus comes in, bundled in a red windbreaker jacket with a scarf around his neck. In fact, all five of them are bundled up.

"Where were you?" I ask, but Lotus speaks at the same time.

"Are you ready? I have a sweet plan for tonight!" He rubs his hands together and gives me a toothy grin.

Julep, who is standing to his right, gives me a cheesy thumbs up.

Haru pops up behind them wearing fuzzy, pale pink ear muffs and a bright yellow jacket that I'm pretty sure has a Pokémon tail on the back.

Starling is inching away toward the dormitory.

"Hold on," Lotus says as he grabs Starling by the arm. "You're coming with us."

Starling turns toward him, a pleading expression on his face.

His hesitancy increases my interest. I stand and button up my trench coat. "Where are we going?"

"It's going to be awesome," Lotus says, his voice boisterous. "I found a race track that will let us drive real race cars. It's the dream."

I can't suppress the grin that comes to my face. "You're kidding." But I'm pumped. I love driving. No, strike that. I love driving *fast*.

"I swear. And the best part? I talked Royal into it by framing it as a training exercise! A training exercise. Who's a genius?"

"It is a training exercise." Royal's voice makes us spin toward him. "And I expect all of you to take it seriously." He's standing in the doorway that leads to the control room, hands resting in the pockets of his slacks.

Lotus's shoulders slump. "Can we at least pretend that it's all for my birthday?" He gives Royal a wide-eyed stare.

A chuckle escapes the older man. "Fine. Knock yourselves out. In fact, I'll meet you all at Abel's for steak afterward."

"Yes," Lotus says, drawing out the word for emphasis. "Now you're talking."

Royal shifts his gaze to Starling, who throughout this conversation has shrunk back against the wall, his head pulled down into his coat so that it appears he has no neck. "Starling?"

At this, Starling stands up straighter. "Sir?"

"Is there a reason you're hiding back there?"

"That's what I wanted to know," I say, my eyes flitting from Royal to Starling and holding there.

Starling shifts on his feet and clears his throat. "I, um... I don't know how to drive."

My eyebrows shoot up. Now, this is a surprise. "You can't drive?"

He sighs as he looks at me. "Never needed to. At the Academy, I..."

"No details," Royal interjects. "Needless to say, you won't be learning tonight. You can ride with Lotus."

At this, Starling steps forward. "If it's all the same, sir, I'd like to ride with Loveday. Lotus seems a little too excited about this, which I find rather frightening."

Lotus guffaws at this and pounds him on the back. "Don't worry, man. I won't kill you."

"All the same..." Starling says, his eyes trained on me.

Okay, I admit it. His accent is pretty hot. I push away the thought. "Sure. You can ride with me."

"Good," Royal says. "And Haru, you can ride with Lotus. Clarity too."

Clarity nods, looking a bit relieved that she won't be driving either.

"Sweet. Let's do this." Lotus is almost out the door when Royal speaks again.

"Lotus?"

"Sir?"

"If anything happens to the people in your car..." Royal's eyes narrow slightly.

Lotus's eyes go wide and he shakes his head. "No, sir. I mean, yes, sir."

One corner of Royal's mouth lifts, and Lotus sags back, relieved. "You're joking? Oh, that's cold."

The sound of my dad's chuckle lingers after he has disappeared back into the control room.

My adrenaline starts pumping as soon as Starling and I are strapped into the race car the track manager has given us to drive. The helmet I'm wearing is snug on my head as I grip the steering wheel tightly. Beside me, Starling is yanking on his seatbelt to make sure it's as tight as it'll go.

"You ready?" I ask.

Seemingly satisfied with the taut pull of the belt over his legs and chest, Starling lets go of the seatbelt and turns his head to look at me. Our eyes lock on each other, and he speaks. "As ready as I'll ever be."

"I won't let anything happen to you."

He exhales without breaking eye contact. "That's nice to hear. I thought you would be glad to have me gone."

I look away from him and out the windshield to where the signal lights on the track glow red. We're waiting for green, which is the signal that the track is ready and we can start driving these puppies. I push my upper lip out with my tongue, thinking about Starling's words.

"Here's the thing. I wanted you gone from the moment you set foot in the Tower, but it's different now." Ahead of our car, the track is lit by hundreds of bright white lights. It almost looks like it's daytime out on the track rather than 19:00. "If Royal is going to keep me out of the field, which I still think is colossally stupid, by the way, I'll need someone out there watching their backs."

"Like me?"

I purse my lips. "Yes, like you."

"Loveday," he says, his voice low and serious. It forces me to look at him.

His brown eyes bore into my green ones.

I duck my chin, but don't look away.

"I promise you, I won't let anything happen to them."

130

"If you do, then I'll kill you."

His smile lights his eyes. "Now that, I believe."

The atmosphere in our car is getting stuffy, so I change the subject. "Why did you offer to drive to the dead drop the other night if you don't know how?"

Starling's gaze is still trained on me. "You looked afraid, and I wanted to help you."

The look in his eyes is too clear, and my heart thumps louder. I clear my throat to speak, but I'm interrupted by the track marshal.

"Car two, are you ready?" The voice sounds through an intercom in the dashboard.

Thankful for the change in subject, I respond. "We're ready."

"You are a go in three, two, one. Go!"

The lights turn green and my foot goes down on the gas pedal, hard. And just like that we're picking up speed, careening forward around the track. My blood flows through me. I haven't felt this alive in weeks.

# Chapter 19

A succession of quick raps on the door to our room jolts my sister and me awake, but unlike her, who rolls stiffly off her mattress with perfect, wavy beach hair, my hair is sticking straight up on one side. I try to press it down, but Clarity's already got the door open, unabashed at the idea of anyone seeing her in the camisole and boxer shorts she sleeps in.

Starling is standing in the dorm hallway, already fully dressed in slim-fit, dark-wash jeans and a creamy camel-colored knit sweater under a navy collared jacket. His eyes widen at the sight of Clarity, but then he catches sight of me, still sitting in bed, my hair sticking straight up. He can't suppress the grin that rises at the sight of me in this embarrassing state. "Nice hair."

"Shut up." I pull my comforter up higher with one hand while trying to press my hair down with the other, to no avail.

"What's going on?" Clarity says as she leans against the door, moving to block Starling's view into our room. A yawn escapes her.

"Royal wants to see us in fifteen minutes."

"It's early," she says.

It dawns on me before Starling can respond, and I leap out

of bed, no-longer caring that I'm only wearing a white, off-the-shoulder tee and Captain America underwear. "He's figured out where The Chin is, or where he's planning to unload the software. Close the door." Rather than waiting for my sister to get her sluggish body into gear, I push the door closed and throw on my personal uniform.

Clarity drags across the room and kneels down to rummage through the clothes she's left strewn over the floor, finally emerging with a heather gray hoodie and a pair of black leggings clutched in her hands. She pulls them on with a groan and stands, blinking to wake herself up.

"You ready?" But I'm out the door before Clarity can respond. I'm barreling toward the control room when an unholy thought stops me in my tracks. Royal won't take the team to Russia without me, will he? I push myself into the control room and sit at the long conference table that runs along the back of the room. Lotus and Starling are already seated. Lotus looks like he's about to fall asleep upright in his chair, but Starling looks bright-eyed and bushy-tailed. Freaking morning person.

Royal steps out of his office and closes the door behind him. In a minute or two, I'll know my fate. I just hope I can stand the wait. He sits at the end of the table, adding a calm, stabilizing presence to the room. I study him, hoping to catch a glimpse of what he's thinking, but he's an impenetrable wall. I can't read anything about him this morning, which is probably not a good sign.

Lotus yawns and rubs his eyes. "It's early, even for me. What's up?"

Royal eyes him before speaking. "Let's wait for Haru and Clarity, shall we?"

The only response Lotus gives is another yawn.

Clarity strolls into the room without a stitch of makeup on. She's got her hoodie tightened over her ears and hair so all that's visible is her square face. She catches my eye. "What? I didn't have time for anything."

"True."

She pulls a chair closer to mine and sits, leaning her head on my shoulder. I wouldn't be surprised if she, too, fell asleep.

I stretch my arms and crack my knuckles. The popping and cracking is loud in the stillness of the control room.

"Does anyone want a toaster pastry?" Haru capers into the room holding a couple boxes of the breakfast goodies. "I've got mixed berry and cinnamon sugar."

"MB for me," Lotus says, nostrils flaring at the sugary scent in the air. Haru gladly hands him a silvery foil packet.

"Cinnamon sugar, please," Starling says. "Thanks!"

"Loveday?" Haru turns to me, holding out both boxes. "Take your pick."

"Everyone knows mixed berry is the best flavor." I grab one and rip it open, taking a big, chewy bite of tart fruitiness.

Clarity alone balks at the idea of eating them cold. "I'll eat when we're done here," she says, lip curled upward.

"Eat something, Clarity," Royal says. "We're leaving as soon as we're finished."

The gravity in his tone perks me up. It's go time. That means the intel Starling and I picked up from his contact at the CIA must have been all the information he needed on The Chin to move forward with our mission to stop him from selling the facial recognition software to the highest bidder, and plunging the world economy into a swirl of identity theft confusion.

"Okay," Clarity says, swallowing. "Wild Berry?"

Haru hands her the packet and plops down in a seat to

munch on her own pastry.

"You got the information you need," I say, leveling my gaze at Royal.

He meets my eyes. "You've got crumbs on your chin."

I swipe them away. "The Chin. Where's he holding his auction?"

Royal purses his lips. "St. Petersburg."

"The Olympics," Starling and I say at the same time.

"It's a great cover," I continue, "with all the extra people there."

"It'll be a zoo," Lotus says through a mouthful of food.

"Chew, swallow, then talk," Clarity says with a tug on the cord of her hoodie. "It's too early for this."

It is early, but I'm surprised Julep isn't here. I glance around the room, but there's no sign of her.

As if reading my thoughts, Royal speaks. "I sent Julep ahead to coordinate with Charles. They'll round up the equipment we need and bring it to the hotel where we'll be staying."

"Let me guess: the Darnay Plaza St. Petersburg."

Royal nods. "I've put Lotus and Starling in a room, and Clarity, you'll share with Julep. Here are your passports. Fake names again. Memorize these."

My heart sinks as I look down at my empty hands. There it is, the answer I've been waiting for. "You're leaving me here." My voice is flat. I can barely control the frustration that's exploded toward the surface of my mind, threatening to overflow like the vinegar and baking soda volcanoes my sister and I used to enjoy making when we were kids and still lived in a normal house above ground.

"Yes, you and Haru are to remain here in the Ivory Tower."

The control room falls silent. The only noise is the occasional chewing sounds coming from my teammates. The majority of my breakfast sits uneaten on the table surface in front of me. I don't have the stomach for it now. My eyes fall to my lap. I can't stand the sight of my dad right now and refuse to look at him.

"Dad?" Clarity speaks up from beside me. "Are you sure that's a good idea? We needed her with us in Port Klang, and St. Petersburg is going to be even more chaotic."

"We know exactly who we're dealing with this time," he says, "And Charles will be there as well."

"But we haven't really worked with Mr. Darnay before," Clarity says. She's pushing it farther than she ever has before, and I love her for it.

"He was here for some of your training. That's sufficient."

"Are you sure?" Starling speaks slowly, as if he's hesitant to voice his thoughts to his superior.

Royal stands. "My decision is final." He scoops up his laptop and holds it against his side. "You've got an hour to pack, and then we're leaving for the airport. Clarity, help Starling pack, will you?"

"Huh?" Starling's eyebrows shoot up.

Clarity smiles. "This is my specialty. No white socks, tennis shoes, jeans, T-shirts, or hoodies." She checks the items off on her fingers.

Royal looks at me, waiting a bit before sealing my fate, as if the pause will give me enough time to prepare for the fact that my life as a teenage spy might be totally over. "Loveday, your shift at the concierge desk starts in two hours. I expect to receive a good report of your work ethic when I return."

I nod, fists clenched under the table. My temporary removal from duty just got extended, indefinitely.

"Loveday, I—," Starling starts.

"Don't," I say. "I can't do this right now." Tears threaten to spill over, so I thrust myself out of my chair and jog through the den to the dormitory. I throw on my running clothes and am out the door before anyone has a chance to say anything else to me. The pressure of the emotions built up inside me is so high I might erupt, and the only remedy is the fast, rhythmic sound of my shoes hitting the pavement.

My feet carry me past George Washington University, past skyward-reaching edifices of red brick and glass, past townhomes with steepled dormer windows, past that great white residence where monumental decisions that steer our country are made. A thought strikes me. I know where I'm going. The renewed feeling of purpose propels me forward. My speed increases as I take in deep breaths through my nose and extend each exhale out my mouth. I'm almost there.

The concrete and glass building rises up to greet me, and I stop under the green, leafy boughs of the trees that line the sidewalk. A glance at my watch tells me it's a little early for them to be open, so I sit on the brick retaining wall that separates the sidewalk from the planters that run the length of the building. The heavy scent of moist dirt fills my nostrils, and I turn to run a hand through the delicate ferns at my back. They're flourishing here in the shade provided by the trees, protected from the harsh morning sun.

My watch beeps.

**Clarity**
**Where are you? We're leaving and I wanted to say goodbye.**

**Me**

**Sorry, I had something to do. Be careful.**

**Clarity**
**Love you.**

**Me**
**Love you too.**

A clicking sound catches my ear. Someone's unlocking the door to the building. I stand and follow her inside. This shouldn't take long.

The air in the Tower is quiet and still when I step inside. I strain for sound but hear none. Haru is probably upstairs with Truly. I walk through the dormitory hallway to the room I share with my sister.

There's a note tacked to my bedroom door. It's written in a scratchy hand I don't recognize.

*I'll take care of them for you. Starling*

My heart constricts. I push inside and close the door behind me, as if confining my crying to my bedroom will make it unreal. If I cry but no one sees, did I cry at all? I tap a message into my watch and send it before I lose my courage.

**Me**
**Thanks.**

It isn't much, but it'll do. I have no idea when he'll get it since he's probably on a plane right now, flying to St. Petersburg.

I sniff.

My eyelashes stick together at the top of my vision as I take in the room I share with Clarity.

There are several wigs missing from the shelves on the wall, and there's a pile of her clothes on the floor. A faint smile crosses my face. That's just like her. She probably debated about what she wanted to bring until the last second.

My watch vibrates.

**Starling**
:)

It's a bit of cheer from the boy who ruined everything. But no, that isn't really a fair statement. It's not fair at all. I'm the one who ruined everything. I didn't speak up when Royal finally let Vale go into the field. And it was me who asked him, of all the people on my team, to back me up when I needed to take down that helicopter. I was the one who let the loss of him eat me up inside until I couldn't ask any of my teammates for help for fear of them ending up dead like Vale. Like Cameron Walker Lewis. I'm the one who ruined everything, and now I'm the one being punished for it.

I stow the government document I've just picked up in the top desk of my drawer, grab my shower gear, and go to the bathroom. I'm almost never here alone, and the silence has my senses on high alert. I try to relax as I step into the hot water, letting it wash away the weight in my soul from being replaced and left behind, made useless. Finally, after weeks of holding them in, the tears flow. Only because there's no one here to see them, to hear my sobs as I realize that my team is about to have an adventure, possibly put their lives at risk, and I'm not there to bring them home safely. I'm not there to take the first step into danger, to forge the strengths of my teammates into an unstoppable force. In this moment I have to trust Starling, Royal, and Julep to bring my team, my family, home, and I don't know if I have the strength in me to do it.

# Chapter 20

Haru closes her laptop with a smack as I walk into the control room. She turns to me with a huge, fake smile.

"What were you doing? Reading something smutty?"

Haru's cheeks turn a flattering shade of red. "No, of course not."

I smirk at her. "Then why the need to keep me from seeing it?" I plop into the desk chair beside her. "Everyone's got their guilty pleasures, you know."

"What's yours?" Haru asks. She's clearly trying to keep me from seeing what she was up to on her computer, but I play along.

"Marvel movies, obviously." I shrug.

Haru giggles. "Those are not guilty pleasures. Everyone in the world loves those. What's your answer, for real?"

"Radish Head," I whisper.

"What? I can't hear you." Haru grins, cupping her hand around her ear.

"Radish Head," I yell.

She squeals. "I'm with you, girl. His costumes are hysterical, and his voice kills me so much. It's truly amazing." Haru gushes, holding her fists up to her cheeks.

I let out a chuckle. "It's true. So." I level my eyes at her. "Are you going to show me what you were doing on your laptop, or do I have to take it from you?"

Haru's eyes widen, but she must catch the glint of teasing in my expression, because she turns serious as she opens the laptop for me to see.

It's a view into someone's living room. White walls dotted with framed floral prints. An old, maroon sofa and a brown reclining chair turned toward a small television. A Japanese man is asleep in the recliner, his head lolled back and his mouth hanging open. There's a cane propped to one side.

I cut my eyes toward Haru. "You're spying on someone?" I can't keep the pride out of my voice, but it's tinged with discomfort. "Who is that?" Then I see it: the family portrait on the wall beside the recliner. It's Haru, her mom, and the man who now sits asleep in the recliner. "Your dad?"

Haru nods. "I like to check in on him every few days."

"So, instead of just doing a video call, you hacked into their computer webcam?"

Haru frowns.

"Don't mistake me. I'm impressed."

She gives me a faint smile. "I miss him so much, and this way I can see how he's really doing." She hesitates. "My mom, she…"

I can sense it in her pause, the reason she's spoken to her dad a bunch over the last few months, but hasn't mentioned her mom. "She talks down to him like she does to you."

"Yeah, she does. She's always so pushy, so negative. After he got hurt at work it got worse. He wasn't able to provide for us anymore so she had to go to work at the hotel. And when that wasn't enough, she made me drop out and go to work with her. It eats him up." She stares at her dad as he sleeps, the

142

remote control on his chest rising and falling with each breath.

I put a hand on her shoulder. "I'm sorry. That's really rough."

She sniffs once, and then flings her arms around my waist and buries her face in the front of my trench coat.

I put my arms around her head and hug her gently. It's awkward, but I don't let go, not until she does.

She's got the imprint of a button on her forehead as she closes her laptop.

"Hey, I'm starving, and there's a killer Japanese grill down the street. You game?"

"Yes!" Haru breathes. "That sounds fantastic."

"Excellent." I follow her through the den and out the service tunnel. I may be banned from the mission in St. Petersburg, but there's still one member of my team who needs me, and I'm going to be there for her, the best I can.


My watch chimes. I open one eye and glance at the screen. It's Clarity, bundled up in a knit sweater, scarf, and knit cap. "What?" I answer, and then yawn.

"You're still sleeping? Your shift at the concierge desk starts in ten minutes."

I sit bolt upright in bed, and my bed head hair brushes the ceiling. "What are you talking about?"

Clarity laughs. "You overslept! You're going to be late."

I rub my eyes with my free hand. "Ugh. You've got to be kidding." I lift my watch to my face and, sure enough, she's right. I have nine minutes to get upstairs.

My sister shakes her head. "Sorry."

"Sure you are." I look past her face, trying to catch a glimpse of St. Petersburg, but all I see are patches of white. "Where are you? How's it going?"

Clarity's smile remains, but it's tighter now. "We're at the hotel, waiting for confirmation that The Chin is where we think he is."

"Where do you think he is?"

Clarity shushes me. "You know I can't tell you." She glances behind her. "Dad's not here or I wouldn't have said even this much."

Lotus pushes his way into view. "Loveday, are you still in bed? Get a move on. Also, you should see the digs Darnay's got us staying in. It's pretty sweet."

"Yeah, yeah." I climb down the ladder and stand in the middle of my pitch-dark room. "How's the food?"

Lotus grins. "I had Russian pancakes with honey for breakfast, and I have to tell you, it was amazing. I am so doing that when I get home."

"You're becoming quite the cook."

Lotus grins, but doesn't have a chance to say anything before Starling pokes his head into view. "Hi, Loveday. How are you?"

I raise my chin in response. "Good. You?"

He gives a wide smile. "This is great." Then quieter. "I wish you were here to see it."

"Don't we all," I deadpan.

Clarity glances over her shoulder. "Oh. Dad's here. Gotta go. Love you."

She hangs up before I can reply. They all look great, and it sounds like they're having a blast in Russia even though they've only been there for a couple of days. What I wouldn't give to be with them right now. Instead, I've got four minutes to get up to the concierge desk. Yay.

Summer is grinning as I approach our workstation. Her

shimmery blond hair is curled around her shoulders, and she's got a killer cat eye going on.

"Someone's alive, alert, awake, and enthusiastic," I say, sliding in beside her.

"You're absolutely right; I am. And you will be too as soon as I tell you what we're doing today." She's so excited she's practically vibrating.

"Okay, I'll bite. What are we doing today?"

"Do you know that super exclusive vegetarian restaurant that opens downtown next week?"

I know exactly what she's talking about. Haru's been going on about it since she got wind of it a few months ago. "You mean the one that grows all of their produce on the roof, so they had to wait until spring so they would actually have food to serve?"

Summer is bouncing now, she's so excited. "Yes. That one! I've been sweet-talking the owner for the past two weeks, and, you know, sending them little gift baskets and things, and this morning I got an invitation to have a tasting with them! Can you imagine how awesome it will be to tell people that we've been there?"

"We're going today?"

"Yes." She looks down at the clock on the tablet in front of her. In just a few minutes."

I glance at my watch. "Isn't it a little early for lunch?"

Summer laughs. "Well, yeah, but this is when they could accommodate us, and I wasn't about to say no."

"Sounds good. All I had for breakfast was a toaster pastry."

Summer pushes herself up to her full height and picks up her whisper-thin phone. "Great! I'll call us a car. It's pouring out there."

I glance out the front door, and, sure enough, she's right. I had no clue. It's one downside of living in an underground bunker—no windows.

# Chapter 21

Royal won't answer when I try to video chat with him to see how everyone's doing. Instead, all I get is a text message.

**Royal**
**Everyone is doing well. Focus on your concierge work.**

Easy for him to say.

I climb up onto my bed and take out the worn document I've been keeping in my pocket.

The same words jump out at me every time I look at it.

*Crushed chest and abdomen.*

*Died on impact with previously damaged guardrail.*

These phrases spin through my brain and ricochet like billiard balls on a pool table. I can't stop staring at my mom's death certificate. The words are there in black and white, leaving white spots in my eyes. But if my mom is dead, why have I seen glimpses of her over the past few months? It's like she's come back as a spectre, rising from the dead to haunt me in my guilt over Vale's death. I would have thought she'd be more comforting, but each time I see her my body goes cold, and my heart stops. I stare up at the smooth, lightly-textured ceiling mere feet above me, willing the weight of foreboding to leave me. It doesn't.

"Loveday!" Haru squeals as she runs down the hall, her feet thudding in slippers shaped like a large, gray tree spirit from one of her favorite anime films. "It worked! We're through Royal's firewall."

My eyes bulge. "Get out," I yell as I jump down from my lofted bed. "We're in?"

Haru's slippers lose traction and she slips, almost falling as she reaches my doorway. A quick reflex to grab the doorframe is what saves her from landing flat on her face on the dull carpet. "I just got the notification," she says, panting. "Wow, that was close." A small titter escapes her as she straightens.

I throw on my trench coat. "Can we access Royal's computer from here? Right now?"

Haru nods, eyes wide.

"Show me."

She takes off like a shot down the hall, through the den, to the control room. Her fingers whizz over her screen as she accesses Royal's laptop, all the way in St. Petersburg. "Isn't unlimited connection a dream?" she says as she works. "Really, how did anyone do anything before the Internet?"

I pull up a chair and slump down beside her, leaning in so I can see her screen. "No idea. So, the software Vale installed finally cracked the firewall?"

Haru shakes her head. "Best I can tell, Royal's antivirus lapsed a few hours ago and he hasn't noticed yet. We may not have much time."

"Then hurry up."

Haru smiles as she splits her screen into two viewing windows. Royal's desktop pops up in the right window. "Okay, we're in. What do you want to see?"

My heart is pounding. I am absolutely certain that I'm

going to find out what my dad is hiding about his adoption of Clarity, and all it will take is a few strokes of Haru's fingers over her screen. "Search for Clarity, her name."

Haru types it into a search window, and then we wait. In only a couple of seconds, a window pops up with the results of the search. There must be hundreds of documents that include her name: training reports, mission debriefs, personal entries Royal has written. It would take us days to wade through it all, and we don't have that much time. As soon as Royal realizes his antivirus software has expired, he'll renew it and we'll be locked out, probably forever. "Here, move over. Let me try something." Haru rolls her chair to the side so I can type on her removable keyboard. "Don't look."

Haru averts her eyes without question. "I'm hungry. I think I'll get a snack." She pops out of her chair and leaves the room. I can hear her steps echo as she descends the stairs into the kitchen. I type in Clarity's name, her real name—Antonia Arnoni—and wait.

The search completes, and there it is: one folder that contains that name. I pause for a moment with my finger hovering over the screen, but I don't hear anything but the distant sound of a cabinet opening and closing. I click on the folder and it springs open. There are dozens of documents saved here. Luckily for me they're organized in reverse chronological order. I scroll to the bottom and my eyes hit on the very document I've been hoping to get my hands on. Clarity's birth certificate. Well, Antonia Arnoni's birth certificate. I open it and scan it quickly. My shoulders slump as I read. It doesn't include any information I don't already have. It's just her parents' names, Carmine and Giada Arnoni, her date and time of birth, the hospital where she was born. Disappointment seeps in. I thought if I could get a look at this thing I'd know what it is Royal isn't telling me, but it looks like a dead end.

I close the file and start looking at the others in the folder, looking for something significant.

Wait.

There's a document that's labeled with the name Giada Arnoni. I look for a file on Clarity's birth father, Carmine, but there isn't one. I guess he didn't bother looking into Carmine once he heard he was in the mob.

I click on the file marked with Clarity's birth mom's name, and my heart slams into my chest. It's an email from Giada Arnoni to my dad, under his real name. Why on earth would she know his real name? I begin to read, and every word is like a knife in my chest.

Does your wife... Have you told her? ...Pregnant. Carmine husband doesn't know... Due next June.... The baby is yours.

"No!" I don't realize I've yelled it out until Haru comes scrambling back into the room carrying a packet of dried seaweed.

"What's wrong? What's going on?"

Bits of dark green stand out on her tongue.

I jump out of my seat, beating back the raging impulse I have to fling the offending device across the room. This is garbage. It can't be true. There is no way that Royal, my dad, would cheat on my mom while on assignment in Italy.

There's no way he would tell that woman, his mistress, his real name and risk exposing himself and his fellow agents, especially to a member of la nostra società.

And there's no way he'd leave a woman who was pregnant with his child alone with a family of criminals and thieves.

But that is exactly what he did.

# Chapter 22

Everything I know about my dad is wrong, and it's tearing me up inside. I thought he was this last bastion of integrity, a good guy through and through. I thought he was honest with me about everything, but now I don't know if I can believe a word he's said.

Clarity isn't just my adopted sister, she's my half-sister. My blood. And he kept it from us this whole time. I'm so livid I wish fire would come bursting out of my head like that cartoon character in that movie about feelings. It would probably help release some of the pressure.

Instead, I stand in the control room, fists clenched, and yell as loud as I can.

Haru shrinks back a little, but doesn't retreat, even though her shifty feet and pale face tell me she wants to. Desperately.

Another yell of frustration escapes me, and my eyes are clamped shut. I take deep, focused breaths in an attempt to calm down. I have to talk to Royal, but I can't come at him with all guns firing. I won't get anywhere that way. Like he's always saying, I have to work on my tact. It's not something that comes to me naturally. I'm more of a shoot now, ask questions later kind of person.

I clear my throat a couple times, and turn to Haru. "I'm sorry about that."

"What's, what's going on?" Her voice is quiet, but sure. She's got more moxie than she lets on.

"I just found out something about Royal that's... not great."

"That's an understatement if I ever heard one."

"Hmph. I can't go into it with you, okay? I'm sorry, but I can't."

She bobs her head. "The secrecy, right? I get it."

"Thanks." I lick my lips. "I need to talk to him. I'll be out in a bit." I stalk to my room and lock the door behind me. I don't want an audience for this.

I plop down in my desk chair and call Royal. Hopefully he'll answer this time. He's been ducking my calls; instead, he replies with short, to the point text messages. He must be pretty busy over there keeping everyone on track.

After a few rings, he answers. "Loveday." The lines across his forehead are more pronounced, and his eyes are tired, but he smiles when he sees me. "How are you?"

"It's nice of you to deign to answer my call," I say, the fury seeping into my voice.

Royal's eyebrows crease. "What's wrong?"

I take a deep breath. "Are you alone?"

He glances behind him. "At the moment."

"You lied to me."

"What are you talking about?" It's not a denial.

"So there are multiple things you've lied about? Not just one big thing?"

He's so calm, so serene, that I want to punch him in his smoothly shaved, age-lined, stupid face.

"How can you sit there all high and mighty, knowing that

you're lying to me, to Clarity, every single day?"

Recognition dawns in his face. "You're the one who installed that malware on my laptop."

"Vale did it for me."

"My antivirus expired a few hours ago."

"Yeah. I know."

Neither of us flinches. It's a stare down, like Clarity and I used to do as kids. She always won with her big, brown doe eyes, but today I refuse to lose.

Royal blinks. It's a slow, deliberate movement. "How much did you see?"

"Enough to know about Clarity's biological parents, and I'm not talking about Carmine Arnoni." I jab a finger at the screen.

He gives a slight nod.

"Why didn't you tell us?"

Laughter sounds behind him, and a door opens. "We're back. Who're you talking to?" Clarity leans over Royal's shoulder, sees me, and grins. "Hey Sis! You wouldn't believe the churches they've got here. They're gorgeous."

"Amazing," Lotus chimes in. "So tall and shiny."

"Great," I say, not looking away from Royal's face. "I'll let you go," my mouth says, but my eyes say something else. They say we aren't done talking about this, not by a long shot.

"We'll talk to you soon," Royal says, and I hang up. The truth about what he did is going to eat me up until he gets home so we can have it out. I want to scream and yell, but I don't want to scare Haru. From what she's said, Haru's heard enough yelling at home to last a lifetime.

My watch vibrates.

**Clarity**

153

**Dad seems flustered. What did you guys talk about?**

**Me**
**I'll explain it when you get home.**
**Focus on The Chin, okay?**
**And stay safe.**

**Clarity**
**Whatever you say, Boss. ;)**

It hurts to lie to my sister, but I can't tilt her axis so far right now. She's got to focus on the mission and coming home safe. There's no telling what she would do if she found out everything I know. I cast around my room for something to do, but nothing appeals. I've got to get out some of the energy that's coursing through me, forcing me to keep moving. When I'm all jumbled up like this, there are a couple of different things that help me unwind. I change into my workout clothes and head upstairs to the hotel gym. There's a punching bag calling my name.

I step into the Tower and take out my headphones and stow them in the pocket at the waistband of my leggings. The blare of metal music is replaced by the upbeat rhythm of J-pop. I follow the music to the control room, where Haru has the projector on and is cycling through surveillance videos and images on the large screen at the front of the room while bouncing around to the music.

She stops when she sees me, her face going white. "You weren't supposed to see these!" She shouts over the music, scrambling to shut down the screens, but it's too late. I've already gotten a good look at the images.

"What are those?" I step toward the screen and squint at the details. The photos and videos are all of a large, mostly empty airplane hangar. There aren't many identifying marks. The only clue that the images weren't taken here in the U.S. is the sign over the exit door. "Wait, these are surveillance from the team in St. Petersburg, right?"

I turn to Haru, who motions for me to give her a second.

Once the music is paused, I try again. "These are from the team in Russia."

"Mmhm. Royal has me running facial recognition using a couple of our databases. He tried to do it from his laptop, but the Internet speed there made it really slow."

"Found anything yet?"

"The Chin hasn't shown up yet, if that's what you mean."

"But they expect him to." I study the screen. There don't appear to be any security cameras in or around the hanger, well, except for the bugs my team planted that took these shots. "It would be a good place for a discrete auction."

Haru nods. "That's what they think too, so they're watching the place. Based on their intel, the auction takes place tomorrow."

That's good news. It means I won't have to kick around here waiting to be let in on what happened for more than another day or two. Then I can stop stressing about everyone. I won't be able to unwind until they're all home safe.

Wait. "Go back. Go back." I'm out of my chair and peering at the screen.

"Okay, hold on." Haru cycles back through the photos.

"Stop!" I hold up a hand as I stare at the screen. My heart is in my throat. There's someone at the hangar who I recognize, and who I never thought I'd see again: Clarity's maternal grandfather, Beppe Arnoni.

# Chapter 23

My legs tremble as I scurry into Royal's office and close the door behind me. Haru doesn't need to hear my conversation. Of course, Royal doesn't answer when I call. I send him a message.

**Me**
**I have to talk to you.**
**Emergency.**

He doesn't respond. Terror rises in me as I call my dad, over and over, willing him to pick up, but I get nothing in return but an empty screen. He probably thinks I'm going to yell at him this time. I mean, I am, just not about what he thinks I'd yell about.

I grunt with frustration as I call him again, and again he declines my call. He's acting like he doesn't have time for me right now, and it's driving me up the wall. My finger hovers over the button that would connect me to my sister, but I hesitate. I don't want to scare her, and knowing that Beppe Arnoni is in St. Petersburg will definitely freak her out. An image of her rises in my mind: her olive skin pale and eyes wide. I can't do that to her.

So I call Starling instead. And like the professional, reliable guy he is, he picks up immediately. "Loveday. I'm surprised to hear from you," he whispers.

All that I can see behind him is white, cloud-covered sky. "Where are you?"

"I'm on a roof across from the place where the auction is being held, you know, surveilling." His warm brown eyes meet mine.

"I already know about the airplane hangar."

"Somehow I'm not surprised."

"I'm not calling about that. I need you to do me a favor."

"I can't give you any more details on our mission," he says. "I'm sorry."

"I don't care about that right now. Listen, we've got a problem."

"And you called me first? I'm honored."

"Ugh. You're so frustrating. Just listen will you?"

He nods. "Okay. Serious time. Got it."

"Finally. I was with Haru when she was running your surveillance footage through the facial recognition software, and I saw…" I trail off, trying to decide what to say. Starling has no clue about Clarity's and my trip to Sicily, or her actual parentage, or anything. Like usual, I take the direct approach. "Clarity's from Sicily. Her parents there were involved in the mob. Her grandfather is a head honcho in their organization, and he's in St. Petersburg. I saw him in the photos."

Starling's eyes are wide as he sets his angular jaw. "Wow."

"Yeah. Look, I don't know if he's there for the auction or if he somehow found out that Clarity is there, but you have to keep her away from this guy." I push a button on my watch and send the photo to him. "You can't tell her he's there. And keep her out of sight. Got it?"

"Yes, absolutely. You can count on me."

"Thanks." I hang up. Right now, I have to trust Starling. Everything in me is screaming at the idea of consigning my sister's wellbeing to a near stranger, to someone who I've spent the last several months actively hating for simply existing in my space, but right now, he's the best help I've got.

I shoot off a message to my sister.

**Me**
**Be careful, okay?**
**And bring your disguise A-game.**

**Clarity**
**Don't I always?**

I step out of the office and look up at the large screen. Instead of a button-down shirt and shorts, the mob boss is wearing a crisp, tailored suit. It hugs his large frame in all the right places, making him seem taller, broader, and not as round as he is in reality. He looks like he's there for the auction. Maybe he doesn't even know Clarity is there and it's a huge coincidence. "Haru, you see that guy?"

"Definitely. Who is he? You seem pretty freaked out."

I give myself a shake. "I can't say, but I need you to scan the footage for every shot of him you've got, okay? It's important."

She stares at me for a moment, not moving.

"Start now."

"Oh, okay." She spins her desk chair toward her computer and gets to work.

Haru works at the computer late into the night, and I'm right beside her, pacing the floor. She hunches farther down in her chair as she inches closer and closer to her laptop screen.

"Anything yet?" I ask.

"I'll let you know when I find something. I've got tons of footage to work through."

I sigh and start pacing again.

Finally, Haru sits up and glares at me. "Look, I know you're concerned, and I'm thrilled to help you, but it's awfully hard to work with you huffing and puffing around the room. Can you pretty please go do something else for a while?"

I clench my teeth to push down the urge to yell at her. Doesn't she know that my closest family member, my sister, might be in mortal danger? I fight for control. Of course she doesn't know, because I can't tell her, thanks to Royal's stupid training on keeping our private lives private. I glance at the clock. Haru's been at this for hours without a break, all for me. "Are you hungry? I'll get us something."

"Sushi sounds amazing right now."

I nod. "I'll be right back." I stride up and out of the Tower, clinging to the knowledge that Royal trusts Starling. He trusts Haru, and he trusts my sister. I should be able to trust them. I have to make that choice. Isn't my inability to lean on my teammates the whole reason I've been benched in the first place?

I make my way up the street to a killer sushi place. Trusting my teammates is part of being a spy, and if I want to continue in this line of work, I have to make that choice, even when it feels like doing that will put the ones I love in great jeopardy. Maybe especially then.

In the morning, I'm actually glad that I have to work concierge. It'll kill some time and be a great distraction while I wait for news from Haru. I'm aching for news from Starling, but keep repeating the mantra, "No news is good news." And it's true: as long as the mission is going as planned, I shouldn't hear from him. For once, it's a good thing that I'm not getting any messages.

The sight of the control room stops me in my tracks. Haru is slumped over her laptop in the same clothes she was wearing yesterday. Japanese energy drinks litter the desk around her. She's eating toaster pastries and scanning videos and photos for signs of Beppe Arnoni.

I put a hand on her shoulder, and she jumps out of her chair.

"Oh! It's you," she says, jittery energy radiating off her.

My eyes narrow. "How much sleep did you get?"

"Not very much," she says. "My brain wouldn't shut off long enough for me to fall asleep."

"So instead you've resorted to drinking these?" I gesture toward the empty, brightly colored cans with one hand.

"Yep!" She sits back down in her chair and huddles over her laptop again.

"Okay. Um, thank you for working so hard on this. You have no idea how much you're helping me."

Her face turns up toward mine and she gives me a bright smile. "I'll let you know if I find anything. Have fun today, Brittney."

I even laugh a little as I make my way to the concierge desk.

"Oh, good. I'm so glad you're here," Summer says as she moves out from behind the desk carrying several shopping bags full of what looks like female superhero party decorations. "We've got a party to prep and we've only got two hours."

"What party? Two hours?"

Summer gives me a tight smile. "I know, but one of our best clients called this morning asking if we could do a superhero party for his granddaughter. Her parents' flight was delayed so he's left with a heartbroken six year old." She holds the bags out to me. "Help me with these? We're heading to the Rose room."

"All right." I follow her up and help her arrange the room how she wants. Pretty soon the white paneled walls are covered with posters of female superheroes in fierce fighting poses. Colorful streamers crisscross the ceiling, and our bags of decorations are almost empty.

"There's one more thing," Summer says. "I think you're going to love it." She tosses a cellophane-wrapped packet to me. "I think this one's your size."

My eyes fall to the floppy package in my hands. It's an Ultra Woman costume.

"You've got the hair for it," Summer says. "I picked Captain Miracle."

"You want me to wear this?" I ask, looking from the costume to her. "For a children's party?"

Summer's gaze falters, but then she straightens to her full height, levels her eyes at me, and nods. "Yes."

"Awesome."

A relieved smile comes to her lips.

The party is well underway and, I have to say, pretending to be a superhero for six year olds is a pretty sweet gig. They huddle around Summer and me asking us to do amazing things like lift heavy presents or give the girls a spin around the room. I'm whirling as fast as I can and loving every second of it. The pixie of a girl I've just finished spinning giggles as I set her down, and wobbles off toward the snack table in a jagged line.

I glance over at Summer, who is posing with her arms flexed, a smile on her face as parents take photos of her with their daughters, each of whom is wearing a different colored cape. It was a last minute addition I thought of, and thankfully there's a party supply store nearby. One of the bellhops was happy to go over there and pick up the capes for us. The tip Summer gave him certainly didn't hurt.

The brassy sounds of my instrumental movie soundtrack playlist bloom in the background as I walk over to Summer. "What's next?"

Summer glances down at the watch she's hidden under her power bracelets. "Cake," she whispers to me. Louder, she says, "Who's ready for cake?"

A chorus of "Me!" fills the room as the little girls flock toward us, smiles on their faces and tiny hands in the air.

"All right, let's move over here, this way." She guides the little girls to the circular tables at one end of the room. "Where's the birthday girl? Why don't you sit right here?" She pulls out a chair, turns it toward the door, and pats it.

The birthday girl, whose black hair is up in tiny braids that crisscross her scalp, hops into the chair with a grin on her face.

In a sneaky move, Summer hits a button on her watch without anyone seeing her, and we both help all of the girls to find seats around the tables.

A quick rap sounds on the door and Summer calls, "Come on in."

The little girls gasp as one of the kitchen staff enters the room carrying a three-tiered cake iced with chocolate frosting and festooned with superhero banners. The entire cake is alit with candles, and I'm not certain the fire alarm isn't going to go off. I glance upward toward the discrete, white, circular panels in the ceiling, but nothing happens.

"Okay, Melinda, blow out the candles!" Summer kneels down beside the birthday girl and helps her blow them out. Everyone cheers as the kitchen staffer moves the cake to a side table to cut and serve it.

I'm about to follow when my watch vibrates.

**Haru**
**I finally got a hit.**
**On the photo of that guy you asked me to look for.**

My heart plummets into my shoes. I move toward Summer. "I have to go," I whisper to her.

She turns to me, a confused look on her face. "Now?"

"I'm sorry." I turn toward the partygoers. "Hi everyone. I've had a great time here with you girls, but I have to go now."

"You have to go catch a bad guy?" one of the little girls asks, looking up at me with an inquisitive expression.

"Something like that," I say, smiling at her. "Enjoy your cake." I'm out of there before Summer can say anything else. The look of disappointment on her face leaves a twinge of guilt, but I can't dwell on that now. I've got to get back to the Tower.

Haru moves aside as soon as I enter the control room. "Here, look through these and see if they help." She gestures toward her laptop screen. Beyond her, the photos of the hangar are still cycling on the big screen. There are more people in and out in these photos, setting up a long table, rows of chairs, and a few lights on stands.

I sink into the chair she's left open for me and stare at the screen. I flip through the photos, but there's not much going on. It looks like Arnoni is simply walking around the hangar, evaluating the place. "Are there any more photos?" I ask.

"A couple more." Haru leans over in front of me and swipes the screen. Three more photos pop up, but they're much the same as the previous ones. But one photo of him outside the hangar stops me cold. I can't believe what my eyes are looking at. It's a photo of Arnoni talking to someone. A woman. I recognize the dark brown hair hanging down her back, curled at the ends, from the few photographs I've seen. Her brown eyes are focused as she talks to the large man. I thought she was dead, and had been for sixteen and a half years, but there she stands talking to a Sicilian mob boss.

My mother.

# Chapter 24

A string of curses flies from my lips as I stare at the photo.

Haru scrunches down beside me and examines the photo. "Who is that?" she asks, turning her face up to mine.

Screw it. I don't want to keep her in the dark. "The man is Clarity's mob boss grandfather. I don't know if he's there for her or what."

Haru's eyes screw up in her face and her mouth forms a small O. "And the woman?"

I swallow as I study the photo. "Hold on a second." I run to my room, scrambling to retrieve the framed photograph of my mom I keep in my desk, and bolt back out to the control room. The frame creaks as I open its back and pop the photo out. My hand shakes as I hold it up to the screen to compare the images. They match. It's her. I can't believe it.

"Is that your mom?" Haru asks, her voice hushed. "I thought she was—"

"Me too," I say. I've just discovered another giant lie Royal has told me. My mind is reeling. I can't do this. I can't just stay here in D.C. while Beppe Arnoni, and my mother, run around St. Petersburg. After several deep breaths, my thoughts begin to slow. Okay, I admit, I do trust Starling. He's a capable spy.

But I'm better.

I pop out of my chair. "I have to go."

"Go where?"

I gesture wildly at the screen. "St. Petersburg. Where else?"

"But you're not supposed to go anywhere near there right now. Royal said you're off the team." Her voice quiets as she speaks, and she withers away from the livid glare I throw at her.

"Don't you think I know that?"

Her eyes are wide. I'm sure I look like Medusa right now. I work to calm my expression. "Look, I'm sorry, but that's my mom in that photo, and she's supposed to be dead. And she's talking to Clarity's grandfather. That can't be a coincidence. I have to go." I lock eyes with Haru, hoping to imbue my voice with the urgency I feel. "Do you understand?"

She stands. "How can I help?"

Her loyalty in the face of my anger is inspiring. "You're the best. Keep going through the photos for any signs of those two people, and forward them to Starling. Tell him to be on the lookout for both of them."

"Okay, but how are you going to get there? I bet the flights are packed because of the Olympics."

"Don't worry about it. I know someone who can help." I just hope I'm right. Before I have a chance to talk myself out of it, I'm climbing the stairs that lead to the waterfall exit. It's the closest route to the concierge desk, and right now Summer is the only one who can help me.

It's 15:00 and the lobby is full of guests checking in to the hotel. Even so, I'm less than cautious when I step out from behind the waterfall and cross the stepping-stones to the side of the pond. My eyes traverse the distance toward the concierge desk and I freeze.

Summer is standing there, watching me, eyes wide. She moves around the counter toward me, her face twisted in confusion.

I hold up my hand to stop her and jog the remaining few yards to the desk.

She looks me up and down, her mouth gaping. "Where did you? How did you?"

I can't mince words. "I'm not an ordinary teenager," I say.

Summer nods, her expression uncomprehending. But it doesn't matter. All that matters now is working quickly.

"Can you get me a private jet to St. Petersburg? It's an emergency."

This statement, my need, cuts through the mental fog surrounding her. She gives me a wide smile, and for the first time I see the real Summer as she rolls up her metaphorical sleeves and gets to work.

I give her the name I'll be using for travel and head back down to the Ivory Tower. I've got identification papers associated with my fake name, but I have to find them in Royal's office.

If it were any other time, I wouldn't have been able to stop mooning over how nice the private plane Summer got for me is, with its silvery-gray plush interior, large, roomy seats, and a personal flight attendant, Kimberly, who is continually bringing me drinks and snacks, but I can't stop freaking out about Beppe Arnoni talking to my mom. The image won't leave the forefront of my mind, even when Kimberly brings me a plate of perfectly chilled shrimp cocktail. I slather the shrimp in cocktail sauce and take a bite. Oh my gosh Kimberly is my new favorite person.

But then my watch buzzes. Haru's messaging me.

**Haru**
**Are you on the plane?**
**How long will it take to get there?**

**Me**
**Yes, and ten hours I think.**

Ten hours. A lot can happen in that amount of time. I rise and ease my feet forward toward the front of the plane, where the door to the cockpit is open. Sticking my head inside, I scan the skies ahead. Night has fallen, so all I can see below us is darkness. "Hey, Pete, how's it going?"

The pilot, a middle-aged man who reminds me of a younger Harrison Ford, responds without turning around. "Great. The sky is clear, and we're set to arrive in St. Petersburg right around 11AM their time."

His co-pilot, an Indian man in his thirties with a nametag that reads Adnan, takes a peek at me before returning to face front.

I tap the side of Pete's chair with my hand. "Can you go any faster?"

Pete glances at Adnan, who merely grunts. "We can bump it up a bit," Pete says. "Get back to your seat and we'll see what we can do."

"Thank you. I really appreciate it." I swivel on my feet to return to my seat, but Pete's voice stops me.

"Er, why are you in such a hurry, anyway? Don't want to miss the synchronized swimming competition?"

"Something like that."

He lets out a chuckle and I take my seat.

I send Starling a message to update him. He's the only one I've told that I'm coming, but I didn't tell him it was because

I'd seen a current photo of my supposedly-dead mom. I shudder at the thought of having to explain that big old mess to him. Besides, it not really his business.

**Me**
**I'm on the plane.**
**Be there in ten hours.**

**Starling**
**Okay.**

He wasn't thrilled when I told him I was on a plane to St. Petersburg. He probably thinks I decided I couldn't trust him, after all, but that's not it. The truth is that catching sight of that photo of my mom has sent me into an emotional tailspin. I'll sell my soul before I miss a chance to see her in person and ask her where she's been all of these years. I absolutely, 100 percent have to meet her. And I also have to tear Royal a new one for keeping the truth from me. I don't know how I can trust him again after this. But it's no use dwelling on it now when I can't do anything about it.

"Hey, Kimberly," I call to the flight attendant, who is settled in the chair across the aisle from me.

She looks up from her tablet with a smile on her face. "Can I get you anything?"

"Is there a way to watch movies on this rig?"

Her smile brightens. "Of course." She produces a remote control from I don't know where and pushes a button. A whirr sounds behind me and I swivel my chair to see a projector screen creeping down out of the ceiling near the back of the plane. "Sweet."

"Isn't it? What would you like to watch?"

It only takes me a second to decide. "Do you have the

latest Captain America movie?" There are like a hundred items on the chronological listing of Marvel movies, and I'm only a third of the way through.

"Of course," Kimberly says. She scrolls through a massive list of movies and selects the one I want.

"Thanks." If I'm going to be on this plane for another nine hours, I might as well cross a couple movies off my list, starting with my favorite superhero of them all.

# Chapter 25

The mid-morning sun pummels the deep blue water to the west of St. Petersburg as the plane approaches, and the glare off the ocean makes it hard to see. Still, I don't look away. I can't. Despite the stress I'm holding in my limbs, the sight of a brand-new-to-me city catches my full attention. It's breathtaking.

Pete brings the plane down much more smoothly than Lotus did, for which I'm grateful. My stomach is already bothering me, and I don't want to upset it further. Once I lock eyes on Clarity I'm confident the sloshing in my abdomen will wane. Thankfully, I'm already at the airport, and the hangar has got to be close by. A quick check of my watch screen tells me it's nearly 01:00 here in St. Petersburg. The auction is set to start in an hour. That's cutting it pretty close.

It's cloudy and cool out as well. I put on my trench coat, button it up, and cinch in the belt. I'm glad I chose charcoal slacks and black shoes.

I tap out a message to Starling.

**Me**
**We just landed.**

# Where are you?

Starling shares his location with me via my watch, and I cross the aisle to look out the window opposite me. It takes me a second to locate the hangar, but it's there, a few hundred yards down the runway near a line of helicopter pads. Opening the overhead bin, I take out my duffle and my weapons case and set them on the plush, dove gray carpet. I unzip my duffle and take out a wig cap, bobby pins, and the wig I borrowed from Clarity's collection. It's a shoulder-length, honey blond wig with beachy waves, and it looks fantastic with my pale green eyes. In a flash, my new hair is in place; I'm basically a wig-wearing expert by now.

Kimberly watches me closely, her interest apparent on her face.

I stand facing her. "How do I look?"

"You look great. Can I get you anything before you go?" She stands a few feet away from me, her eager face at the ready.

"Can you grab a couple water bottles for me?"

Her countenance brightens, and she heads to the back of the plane where the small wet bar is located. In a blink she's back, holding two chilled bottles out to me.

"Thanks. You're the best," I say as I bend down and stow the bottles in the side pocket of my duffle bag.

At this, the flight attendant inclines her head to one side, her cheeks a rosy pink. "You're welcome."

I scoop up my luggage and walk up to the cockpit. The scrape of my woven duffle bag against the doorframe announces me, and Pete swivels in his chair to meet me. His eyes widen at the sight of my new hairdo, but he doesn't say anything.

"Thanks, Pete, for bringing me." I duck my head to show my appreciation.

"My pleasure, Brittney." His gaze travels down to my weapons case and back up to my face, but his expression betrays none of his thoughts. "Are you staying here in St. Petersburg for the full two weeks of the Olympics?"

"I'm not sure yet. It'll depend on what events I can get tickets for this close to the opening ceremony."

Pete's eyebrows twitch upward, and a crooked smile comes to his lips. "You're not kidding." He pulls a card out of his pocket and hands it to me. "We'll be here for at least eight hours. If you need anything, let us know."

I send Starling a message that I'm on my way.

**Starling**
**Meet me on the west side of the hangar.**

**Me**
**Where is everyone else?**

**Starling**
**Clarity is in a vehicle nearby getting into her disguise.**
**Royal and Julep are with her.**
**Lotus is on the roof.**

**Me**
**You were supposed to keep her away from the auction.**

**Starling**
**Have you ever tried arguing with her?**
**It's not easy.**
**I'm pretty sure she thought I was wary of her being in the field because she's a girl, which is not true.**

This brings a nervous laugh to my lips. The mental image of Starling sparing verbally with my sister is pretty entertaining. I'd like to see it sometime. Of course, that will depend on me keeping Clarity away from Beppe Arnoni. Fear squeezes my heart and I pick up the pace—I'm running down the tarmac toward the side of the hangar, my duffle and weapons cases thumping against my sides.

Even from this far away, I can't see Lotus on the roof. There are short, rectangular boxes at regular intervals along the roofline, which must be skylights. He must be tucked in between them, away from the edge and out of sight.

The hangar opens to the right, and already there are several fancy cars parked on the asphalt. A white catering van with the company name scrolled on the side is parked off to the left, but I don't see anyone near it. They must already be inside the building. I'm thankful for that; it makes it much easier to approach without being seen.

My watch buzzes.

**Lotus**
**What are you doing here?**

I'm not at all surprised that he's spotted me. That's kind of his job, and why he's been posted on the roof.

**Me**
**I'll explain in a minute.**
**Meet me behind the airplane hangar, to the west.**

**Lotus**
**Will do.**

My pulse is quick as I whip around the corner of the hangar.

Starling is already there waiting for me, his back pressed up against the corrugated metal structure. "You're here," he says as he pushes off the wall and stands at full height.

"I'm here." A salty sea breeze picks up the honey-gold strands of my wig and they float across my face. Reaching up with one hand, I place the hair behind my ears before setting my bags on the rocky ground.

Starling looks out at the field to our left, and I follow his gaze. The crisp scent of the ocean wafts by, along with the floral scent of the bright pink and orange wild flowers in the vast field before us.

"Why did you come here?" His dark brown eyes are full of questions as he searches my face, but my expression gives him no answers.

I suck my bottom lip into my mouth as I consider what to tell him.

"You don't trust me." His face is drawn, and disappointment shows in his scrunched eyebrows. It's not easy, but I don't flinch or look away.

"It's not that. I—"

A metal ladder behind Starling begins to rattle.

My eyes follow the length of it up to the roof, where Lotus is maneuvering down from the top of the hangar.

Starling and I stand in silence, watching Lotus's descent. Once he's a few feet from the ground, he jumps, landing with a quiet crunch. "What's going on?" Lotus asks, his attention on me.

"I'll tell you, but I have to make it quick. We don't have time for questions."

"Tell me about it. The auction starts in 40 minutes, and

some of the guests have already arrived."

"Who? Describe them."

Lotus's mouth hangs open as he scratches the back of his neck. "Um, a white male, around eighty years old, in a wheelchair, and his wife, I think. A really buttoned-up white woman, also about eighty, in a floor-length, camel-colored trench. A couple white guys in suits."

"How old are the guys? Was one of them overweight?"

Lotus shakes his head. "No. They're both youngish, and trim."

"Okay, here's what's going on." I pause, my eyes flicking from Lotus to Starling and back. "Clarity's biological grandfather, who is a mob boss in Sicily, is here. I don't know if he's here for the auction or to grab her, but I couldn't take the chance."

"So I was right," Starling says, his eyes boring into me.

"No, I just, I can't tell you the rest."

He frowns and trains his gaze on the ground. "Fine."

Lotus raises an eyebrow at me as if to say, "Really?"

I purse my lips in response. "Once we're done here I'll explain everything, but we don't have time right now." I call up the photo of Arnoni and my mom on my watch and show it to them. "If you see either of these people, let me know immediately. Okay?"

Both guys nod in assent.

"Thanks. Now, get back to your posts. I'm going to find the others."

"Yes, ma'am," Lotus says as he steps onto the ladder and proceeds to climb aloft to the roof.

Starling merely gives me a curt nod before turning and walking around the corner of the hangar.

My watch pings. Starling has sent me a dropped pin of the

location of the van.

I skirt along the hangar wall back toward the parking lot, and peek out once I reach the corner. The oversized airplane door isn't open, so the only point of entry is the standard-sized door at the opposite corner.

An elegantly dressed elderly woman has the gall to stand waiting for the gentleman approaching from a few feet away to open the door for her.

A quick scan of the parking lot reveals that there aren't any occupied cars, and no cars on approach. I'll have to cross a bit of open space to get to the spot where Royal has parked the van at the far end of the lot, about a hundred yards away, but I probably won't be seen. I redirect my attention to the drama at the hangar door.

The gentleman finally reaches the door and holds it open for the lady, who says, "Finally," in a shrill voice. The man rolls his eyes but says nothing as the lady sashays inside, her high heels clacking on the concrete. Once their backs are to me, I start across the parking lot at a leisurely pace. Experience has taught me that I'm more likely to attract attention if I'm obviously in a hurry to get somewhere. Instead, I move toward the back of the lot at an amble, my bags swinging at my sides and a relaxed expression on my face.

I'm almost to the van when the side door slides open and Julep steps out wearing a white button-up shirt, a thin black tie, and black slacks—the universal signifier of catering staff.

"Honey, I'm home," I say as I close the gap between us.

Julep moves to one side, gesturing with her arm for me to step into the vehicle, an amused look on her face.

I slide my bags inside and step up. It's one of those cargo vans with a cabin large enough to stand in.

Across from me, there's a narrow shelf that runs the

length of the van, and on it sits a flat computer monitor showing a video feed of the inside of the hangar, its exit door, and the parking lot.

"You saw me coming," I say, turning to Royal, who is standing a couple feet from me, arms crossed.

"And that comes as a surprise to you?"

"No."

Julep sticks her head in. "I'm gonna get into the hangar. My catering shift starts in five minutes."

I look down at my watch. It's thirty minutes to auction time.

"Go ahead." Royal waves her off.

There's a shuffling sound behind Royal as Clarity pushes around him wearing a chin-length, scarlet red, curly-haired wig and a black, sleeveless dress. She presents her back to me. "Zip me up?"

"Nice to see you too," I say, doing her bidding.

She faces me and puts on large, black, cat eye sunglasses. "What do you think?"

Eyeing her up and down, I can't help but think that she looks like a certain red-headed marvel character, who also happened to be a spy. "You look fantastic, but you're sure going to stand out. Can't you wear something a little less noticeable?"

She grins. "I'll take that as a compliment. And anyway, I'm supposed to be Anzhelina Fedorchenko, a Russian diplomat's daughter." She picks up her watch off the desk surface and shows me a photo.

"You look just like her."

"That's the idea."

I turn to Royal. "Let me go in with her. I can be her assistant."

"No. Julep will be inside the hangar if anything happens."

"I'll go after them as soon as you turn your back."

His mouth forms a thin line. "We don't have time to argue about this."

"Come outside with me for a second. Please?" I climb down out of the van and walk around to its nose, which faces away from the hangar.

From inside, I hear Royal say, "Clarity, keep an eye on the monitors. I'll be right back."

Once he's standing a couple feet in front of me, he stops, arms crossed over his chest. His white button-up shirt is rolled up to his elbows and his gray slacks are creased form where he's been sitting in the van for the last several hours. "Why are you here, Loveday?"

I tap my watch and show him the photo I showed Lotus and Starling.

Royal looks down at the screen, and the color drains from his face. His eyes rise to meet mine.

"That's why I'm here," I say, dropping my arm to my side. "And the man is Clarity's grandfather. You know, the one in la nostra società."

"Hmm." He leans back against the van's grill, mulling over this information, face drawn.

"Dad," I say, stepping toward him. My voice comes out in a whisper. "I thought she was dead. You told me she was dead." My mind is spinning. Why would he have told me she was dead if she wasn't? Was the accident a cover-up for something else? Did it even happen? No, I stop myself. I've seen the photos. But photos can be doctored. "Did you make it all up?" I can't keep the frantic energy from my voice.

"Of course not. I would never lie to you about your mother."

"But then how do you explain this?"

Royal drags a hand down his face. "Let me see that photo again."

I hold my watch next to his to transfer the photo to his screen.

He peers down at the screen, then lifts his gaze to the airway beyond us.

I try to catch his gaze, but his eyes have an unfocused, faraway look.

The quiet stretches out between us, but I don't fill it. Instead, I wait for Royal to speak. Finally, he turns his face toward me, his features tight. His voice is low as he says, "She is dead. I don't know who this is, but it's not your mom."

"I have to be sure. Let me go into the auction with Clarity. If she shows, I want to see her."

A ragged breath escapes him. "All right, but don't engage her." He trains his cool blue eyes on me. "I mean it." With that, he moves back around the van and climbs inside.

I don't move. My feet and legs feel as if they're shooting roots down through the asphalt to the earth below, holding me in place. If the woman in the photo isn't my mom, if it's not her who's been shadowing me for the past few months, then who is it?

"Loveday," Royal calls from inside the van. His clipped voice breaks the spell that's fallen over my feet, so I scurry back inside the van and stand behind Clarity, who's sitting on a stool in front of the monitors, legs daintily crossed to one side. Her sunglasses hang from the scoop neck of her dress.

She swivels on the stool and smiles. "So, Dad caved."

The sight of her sitting there with such a gleeful expression almost makes me forget the reason I came here. Almost, but not quite. But I can't tell her about it all right now. What a mess.

My sister must see something flit across my face, because she rises from her seat and leans down to meet my face. "What's wrong?"

"Nothing."

She raises an eyebrow in disbelief, but doesn't say anything. Then, she gives me a once over. "You can't go into the auction in those clothes. Did you bring anything else?"

"Duh." I squat beside my duffle bag, unzip it, and pull out a navy shift dress and black flats. "How about this?"

"Perfect. You'll be my assistant. Now hurry and get dressed. We need to get inside."

I crawl into the front passenger seat of the van and make sure the sun visor blocks anyone from seeing into the van. Then I change as quickly as I can. I'm in the middle of shimmying into my dress when my watch vibrates.

## Lotus
**Arnoni is here, but I don't see the woman.**

I scramble out of the seat, my dress hanging off my shoulders unzipped, and peer at the monitors. Sure enough, Arnoni is strolling into the hangar, alone. Slowly, he reaches up and takes off his sunglasses, folding them and putting them in his jacket pocket.

Behind me, Clarity gasps. "Is that who I think it is?"

I gulp, and, without removing my eyes from the screen, say, "That's exactly who you think it is. But I don't know if he's here for the auction, or—"

"For me." Her face is pale and her doe eyes are wide. "You knew he was coming, and you didn't tell me?"

"I'm telling you now, and besides, him being here doesn't change anything." It's a whopper of a lie if I've ever told one, but I'm hoping it'll calm her down.

It doesn't.

Clarity wraps her arms around herself and stares at the monitor, chewing on her bottom lip.

I glance at Royal, whose eyes are locked on Clarity's face, on the fear apparent in her expression.

Hurriedly, I pluck my sister's sunglasses from the front of her black frock and push them onto her face. "It's okay. I'll be with you the whole time. Just don't take your sunglasses off. He won't recognize you in this." It's most likely true. Clarity looks like a completely different person than she did on our trip to Sicily—her wig, sunglasses, and clothing make sure of that. Plus, I'll be with her to protect her if Arnoni starts to sniff in her direction. But that's not the primary reason I want to go inside. The truth is that despite my dad's assurance that the woman I've seen is not my mom, I don't quite believe him. The hope that she is alive blooms and grows, stretching wide, filling me up with the warmth of it. If she's here, I'm going to see her myself, and maybe even talk to her.

"Girls." Royal's voice is cool, and my heart drops.

We both spin to face Royal, who stands between us and the exit door. "I've changed my mind."

My eyebrows quirk upward. "What?"

He levels his gaze at me. "We're here to stop The Chin from selling that software hack, not to tangle with ghosts from our pasts." The way he lowers his voice when he says the last few words hints that he's struggling with this.

"Ghosts?" Clarity asks, confusion on her face.

I open my mouth to reply, but Royal raises a hand to stop me. "I'm not finished," he says.

I clamp my mouth shut, and he continues. "Arnoni's presence here is too big a risk. You two will remain here in the van. I will attend the auction instead."

"No!" The word bursts out of me before I can stop it. "That's not fair. I want to see her with my own two eyes and not through a stupid monitor."

"See who?" Clarity asks, not looking away from the screens.

Royal shakes his head. "I'm not arguing with you about this. Our mission is of utmost importance." He pauses and lifts his hands, resting one on Clarity's right shoulder and one on my left shoulder. "But it's not as important as my two girls. Now, please, stay here."

A pout rises to my lips, but I say nothing.

To my right, Clarity sinks onto the stool, her body relaxing. Clearly, she's relieved at this turn of events.

Royal kneels down before her and opens a small drawer.

I crane my neck to see inside, and am met with a small, metal case lined with styrofoam. Inside the case are miniscule pairs of earbuds, arranged in two rows. Four pairs are already missing, leaving behind faint indents in the foam.

Carefully, Royal picks up two earbuds in one hand, and then kneels before Clarity, putting his free hand on her knee.

She lifts her eyes from the floor to meet his.

"Be the cord that binds us." He opens his hand and holds out one of the earbuds.

In a slow motion, Clarity reaches up and wraps her fingers around it.

Then, to me, Royal says, "Be our eyes." He shoots a pointed look toward the monitors, and gives me the other listening device. Then he rises to his full height. Reaching toward the driver's seat, he retrieves a sharp, navy suit jacket that had been draped over the arm of the chair. He dons it carefully, and then speaks as if into thin air. "Change of plans, team. I'm bidding in the auction instead of Clarity. She and Loveday will remain in the van." He steps down from the vehicle before turning to us one last time. "Loveday, stay in the van."

I gesture toward Clarity. "Why not tell her to…" But he's already striding across the parking lot toward the airplane hangar.

I let out an exasperated sigh as I slide the van door closed and lock it in place.

Clarity spins on the stool to face the monitors, her eyes flitting from one view pane to the next. Hangar door. Interior of the hangar from below. Interior of the hangar from the skylight where Lotus is stationed. Parking lot. Repeat.

I pull a black case from under the narrow desk and sit beside her, training my eyes on the screens. "What's the plan?"

"I was supposed to win the auction and grab the software from The Chin, but I suppose Dad will do that now."

"That's right." Royal's voice sounds through our earbuds. Over our video feed I can see him strolling across the parking lot and into the airplane hangar. We listen as he checks in to the auction.

"Have fun," I say sarcastically.

He doesn't respond to my bait. He never does, and it's really frustrating. Sometimes I wish he'd just get into a screaming match with me. It would be a lot more cathartic than his usual reaction, which is clamming up completely.

The sounds of cars pulling into the lot fill my ears as they show up on the screen. "Here we go," I say, not bothering to keep the frustration from my voice. Small parties of people exit their cars and walk toward the hangar. They glance at one another as they walk, probably sizing up their competition. One or two greet each other, but mostly they remain silent. "Six more heading your way." I enunciate each word for my teammates.

Clarity gives me a half smile, still clearly relieved about being safe in the van rather than inside. "The auction starts in fifteen minutes," she says. Then, we both focus on the monitors.

# Chapter 26

A navy luxury sedan pulls into the parking lot and comes to a stop right outside the hangar. A uniformed driver gets out and swings open the back door. The Chin steps out, looking snazzier than he's looked in any of the photos we'd dug up of him. Instead of a T-shirt and jeans, he's wearing an electric blue suit. A lanky, bespectacled man climbs out of the car behind him, standing and adjusting his suit jacket. He bends to retrieve something out of the car—a small gavel. It's the auctioneer.

I keep my voice all business as I update everyone. "The Chin is here. He's heading inside, along with his auctioneer."

The man steps into the building.

Over the comms, Lotus laughs. "He'll certainly be easy to keep track of in *that*."

The front passenger door of The Chin's car opens and a security guard, also wearing a suit, a black one, steps out. He trots to the door and stands facing the parking lot. He's wearing both a waist holster and an ankle holster, but he doesn't retrieve either weapon. Instead, he cracks his knuckles before crossing his arms over his chest.

"The Chin has stepped up his security," Clarity says.

"You're not kidding," I respond. And it's true. We've

never seen him with an armed guard in any of the surveillance we've done. The information we've gotten from the CIA says that he's been involved mostly in trafficking goods through the black market, up until now. It appears that he's trying to get in with the big dogs, and the auction of the facial recognition software seems to be the way to do it.

"Here we go," Royal says from inside. "He's making his way up to the front."

"Got your paddle ready?" I quip.

Lotus snickers, but Royal is silent.

I find him on the video feeds of the inside of the hangar. He's standing behind the crowd of people, hands clasped in front of him. And, sure enough, he's got a paddle in one of them.

The auction is about to start and there's no sign of the woman who may or may not be my long-dead mother. Anxious energy courses through me, and I tap a rhythm on the floor of the van with both feet in an effort to be rid of it.

Clarity reaches over and places a hand on my knee. "Please stop."

I still, shooting a half smile in her direction, before training my eyes on the monitors again. If my possible mom shows up, I've got to talk to her, no matter what Royal said. He has no idea what it's like to be without a parent for so long, and then discover that she might be alive and well and within my grasp. Surely it won't hurt anyone if I leave the van, just for a minute.

"Look," Clarity says, patting my forearm with one hand and pointing to the screen with the other.

I follow her finger to its end. She's pointing at Arnoni. "What?" I ask.

"I don't think he's here for the auction," she whispers. "He's not even listening to The Chin. He keeps checking his watch and looking toward the door." Her eyes rise to mine. "Do you think he's looking for me?"

I study Arnoni for a second, and my sister is right. He seems wholly uninterested in The Chin, who's up front monologuing about how the software he's about to sell could be used to get money, lots of money.

"Whoa," Lotus says through the earbuds. "Are you seeing this?"

"What?" I ask, my eyes combing over the monitors.

"Parking lot," he says, voice tight.

I focus on the video feed of the parking lot, and my eyes almost jump out of their sockets.

Charles Darnay is cruising into the parking lot on a flashy red motorcycle.

"What is he doing here?"

"Who?" Starling asks over the comms.

"Darnay," I respond.

"Charles is here?" Royal asks, his voice lifting in relief.

"Yes, Darnay is pulling into the parking lot on a motorcycle. Any idea why he'd be here?"

All I get in response is a, "Hmm."

Darnay parks his motorcycle and swings off it with ease. And then he's striding toward our van.

"He's coming this way," I say. "What do we do?"

"Let him into the van," Royal says. "Ask him what he wants."

"Sure," I say, reaching behind me to unlock the van and push the button that slides the door open automatically.

Darnay rounds the vehicle and sticks his head inside. His eyes widen when he sees us. "Ladies." I wasn't expecting to meet you here."

"Royal's inside the hangar," Clarity says in a welcome voice. "Climb on in."

"Don't mind if I do," he says as he steps up into the van and pulls up a crate behind us. "Has the auction started yet?"

"No," I say, my voice flat.

"Give him an earbud," Royal says.

"Nope," I say, lips curling in distaste.

"Loveday."

I glare at no one in particular and open the drawer to retrieve an earbud for the intruder. "Take these," I say, shoving the tiny piece of tech at him.

Darnay takes it with a grin and puts it in place. "Thank you."

He either doesn't see or chooses to ignore the fact that I'm glowering at him.

"Fill me in," Darnay says, and Clarity obliges.

"Everyone is in place. Lotus on the roof, Starling is watching the perimeter, and Dad and Julep are inside. Dad's going to win the auction and subdue The Chin. It's pretty straightforward."

Darnay inclines his head to one side. "Why aren't the two of you in on the fun, eh?"

Clarity opens her mouth to explain, but I interrupt. "None of your business."

"Loveday," Royal growls through the earbuds.

"No, it's fine," Darnay says, leaning back on his crate and propping his hands on his knees. "I'm just here to observe. Carry on. And just ignore the fact that I'm here, won't you?" He reaches out a hand to pat my shoulder, but I recoil, and he pulls back.

It's one thing to interrupt a game of paintball, but it's quite another to interrupt us when we're on a job. Where does

Charles Darnay get off, and when do we get to that stop?

"This is exciting," Darnay says, leaning between Clarity and me to check the monitors. "I haven't been on a job in a long time." The hairs on the back of my neck stand up as his hot breath grazes my skin.

"Sit back, would you?" I snap. "I can't focus with you sitting there."

Darnay's eyes go wide, but then a sly grin appears on his smug face. "I know it's a lot to have an old-timer like me in here with you, but I promise I'm not critiquing you. I'm just here to see how Royal's team works. I've been wanting to see it since London."

"So you thought you'd drop in on us unannounced in the middle of a mission?" I shoot a glare over my shoulder at him.

Clarity nudges me with her elbow. "Focus."

I exhale loudly and return my eyes to the video feeds. My sister is right; I can't let Darnay get under my skin any further than he already is, especially not right now.

Fortunately, the auction is going well. The participants are bidding casually, and the price for the software keeps rising in small, steady increments. Royal hasn't even started bidding yet. He's feigning disinterest, but I know that once the bidding heats up he'll pounce.

Arnoni is leaning back in his chair, seemingly relaxed. He's trying to appear wholly indifferent to the proceedings. That, or he actually is unconcerned with the goings on around him. It's the latter possibility that worries me. His frequent glances down to his watch belie the relaxed impression on his face. I'm starting to think Royal was right to order Clarity and me to stay in the van. The last thing we need is for this mission to go sideways like Port Klang did. The sensation of Vale's warm blood on my hands rises unbidden and I shove it down. There's no time for that right now, either.

Aside from the mobster, everyone else in the hangar is getting more anxious. People are sitting forward in their chairs, scooching to the edges of their seats, and raising their paddles higher with each bid. The increments have started to grow, and several bidders are edged out of the competition by the elegant mare we saw earlier and a middle-aged man who owns one of the largest oil refineries in Ghana. I have no idea what he'd want with the software, but it doesn't matter. He won't get it.

Finally, Royal raises his paddle to begin bidding.

With a flick of her wrist, the mare outbids him.

Then, the oil tycoon bests her.

The Chin is standing off to the side taking photos of the action on his phone, a wide smile on his face.

The bidding speeds up even more. The three of them are bidding so quickly I can't understand a word of what the auctioneer is saying as it feeds through Royal's earbud and into my eardrum. My eyes are fastened on the video feed. I can't look away. The auction is riveting, even though I already know the outcome. Royal will win at all costs. Unfortunately for The Chin, he'll never see a dime of that money.

First, the Ghanaian man drops out of the race. He sits back in his seat, shaking his head slightly, lips puckered in disappointment. I have to say, I'm surprised. Their economy has exploded in the last decade, mostly due to their brand spanking new oil refineries.

But the older woman isn't having it. She's bidding as fast as she can, and upping the increment every single time.

Royal responds in kind, and she actually glares at him.

The sight makes me want to chuckle. I haven't seen a senior citizen glare at Royal maybe ever. Usually they're thanking him for holding the door open or for some other mundane nicety. But I hold it in. It would not be a good time to interrupt Royal's concentration.

Clarity, too, is smiling at this exchange. Our eyes meet for a fraction of a second before we return our focus to the monitors.

It's over. Royal has won, and his biggest opponent is click-clacking out of the hangar, mumbling to herself angrily. She throws the hangar door open, and it smacks back against the wall, reverberating with a sharp, metallic clang.

Slowly, the rest of the crowd rises from their seats. Some exit the hangar while others make their way to one side of the room where a long table of hors d'oeuvres has been set up. Julep is there smiling at everyone and gesturing for them to try the range of meat cuts, breads, salad cups, and more that are laid out on the white tablecloth.

The Chin stands at the front of the room whispering to the auctioneer, waiting for Royal to approach him.

Royal, for his part, wanders over to the snack table to pick up a bite. He's stalling, waiting for everyone else to leave before he engages The Chin.

After several minutes, all of the auction attendees have vacated the hangar but Royal and Arnoni. Arnoni is sitting in his seat smoking a cigar.

"That stinks," Lotus says through the earbuds. "Do you smell that Starling?"

"Nope," Starling responds, a smile in his voice.

"Lucky," Lotus whines. "It beats me why anyone would smoke those things. They're disgusting."

"They're an acquired taste," Julep intones. On the video feed, I can see her covering her mouth with her hand.

"You *smoke?*" Lotus says, shock apparent in his voice.

Julep does laugh at this. "No, at least, not regularly. It was a big thing at my last job. Ask me about it sometime." Her sly mention of the CIA has me thinking of Julep and a bunch of guys in suits, sitting around an office smoking while they type away at their computers. I crack a smile.

"Hey," Clarity says, bringing my mental focus back to our task. "He's making a call."

Sure enough, Arnoni is standing from his chair and meandering toward the hangar exit, phone in hand. He steps outside and stands upright in the narrow strip of shade that runs along the edge of the building facing the parking lot. The security guard who has been standing sentry for the entirety of the auction scoots away from him along the wall, unsubtly waving his hand in front of his nose. He doesn't like the smell of cigar smoke either. Arnoni smokes on, unfazed by this obvious display of disdain at his puffing. He walks away from the hangar across the parking lot before bringing his phone to his ear.

Inside, Royal is moving toward The Chin.

"Congratulations!" The Chin says in a high nasal voice. It's a thin, reedy sound that doesn't go with his solid appearance. He juts out a hand toward Royal, who studies it a moment before responding in kind.

"Thank you," Royal says as the two men break their handshake. "Do you have the software here?"

"Of course," The Chin beams. "Do you have payment ready?"

Royal lifts his watch and taps a button. "It's ready to send as soon as you tell me where it's going."

The Chin rattles off a bank routing number and account number, and Royal makes a show of inputting the information into his watch screen.

The Chin reaches into his pocket for his phone and checks the screen. "I've just received it. Thank you." He replaces the phone in his jacket.

"The software?" Royal asks.

"Right." The Chin produces a small external drive from an inner jacket pocket. He snaps at the auctioneer, who scrambles to produce a laptop from behind the lectern. He plugs in the external drive and steps aside for Royal to study the screen. "To demonstrate, let's look someone up," The Chin says, rubbing his hands together. "How about you?"

Royal gives him a steady stare, and The Chin takes a tentative step back. "Okay, we'll do me instead." He gives a nervous laugh. "Watch." He stands with his face mere inches from the computer screen for a second, and then steps back. "It'll only take a minute. See?" He stands aside.

Royal reads the screen and looks up to The Chin. "This is you? These are your bank accounts?"

"That's them," The Chin says. "And, watch. You can input a different photo into the software. It'll be uploaded to the CIA's secure database, and you can access the account of whoever you want, using your very own face." He reaches out to pat my dad's cheek, but thinks better of it at the icy look Royal gives him.

Royal nods slowly. "Does the software have any limitations?"

"Nope." He hesitates. "Well, you have to have a photo of the person whose identity you want to steal…" He trails off.

Royal gives a curt nod and The Chin hands over the external hard drive.

"Okay then. It was a pleasure doing business with you, Mr.…."

"And you," Royal says. He turns and ambles across the

hangar.

"I've got a clear shot," Julep says through the earbuds.

"Take it," Royal says in a low voice.

In a second, a tranquilizer dart hits the auctioneer in the shoulder and he crumples to the floor.

"What the?" The Chin says, turning toward the prostrate man with wide eyes. He scoops up his laptop and makes for the door, but a tranquilizer hits him in the center of the back, and he too falls to the ground.

Royal doubles back and lifts The Chin's hands onto his back, handcuffing them in place. "Target is secure."

"Nice," Darnay says from behind us, his voice full of enthusiasm.

"I'll grab the security guard," Starling says. "Am I clear?"

"You're clear," Darnay says.

Ignoring him, I respond to my teammate. "Arnoni is the only one still here, and I don't think he'll hear you from across the parking lot. Go ahead."

Starling makes a bird call sound. I don't know what type, but it definitely doesn't sound human. I wonder if that's why he chose the name Starling. Maybe he's actually into birds. I make a mental note to ask him later when we're not working.

Through the video feed, the security guard perks up and steps around the building, out of sight.

"Hi," Starling says through the earbuds. "You were expecting me?"

"Who are you?" The security guard asks.

A tranquilizer gun fires its telltale whizzing sound.

"Got him," Starling says.

On the video feed, I see a car approaching the parking lot. "Incoming," I say. "One black sedan approaching the parking lot. Starling, are you out of sight?"

Starling grunts in response. "I've almost got my guy into the field. Just a second."

"Get him there, and stay down," I say.

"Got it."

Scuffling sounds come through the earbud, and then it goes quiet. "I'm covered," Starling says.

My eyes are focused on the car as it pulls into the parking lot and skims to a stop beside Beppe Arnoni. He stands facing the car, barely heeding it, and takes a whiff of his cigar.

The back door opens and a woman climbs out. She straightens, and that's when I realize it's her. My mom.

A shiver shoots down my arms and I can't stifle the gasp that rises in my throat.

"Loveday, are you seeing this?" Lotus breathes. "That woman is here to pick up Arnoni."

"What?" Clarity asks, but her mouth drops open when her eyes lock on the video feed. She grabs for me without taking her eyes off the screen, and finally succeeds in twisting her fingers around my upper arm.

"I see her." I eke out the words. From the photograph, I knew she had spoken to him, but it could have been a huge coincidence. It's obvious now that it wasn't. Somehow, my mom is tied to the Sicilian mob.

Behind us, Darnay goes still. After a moment, he whispers. "Who is that?"

"Shut up," I say, pushing myself back from the desk and standing, not taking my eyes off the image of her.

Arnoni gestures roughly toward the hangar with one arm. His features twist in anger and he scowls at the woman. Jabbing a finger in her face, he leans in, whispering angrily.

"What's happening?" Royal asks.

No one responds. We're all too busy watching the drama

that's playing out in front of our eyes.

The woman pales before Arnoni's imposing figure and takes a step back. She holds her hands up in supplication, pleading with him in words we can't hear.

"That looks intense," Lotus says. "Yikes."

"Someone tell me what is going on," Royal demands.

"My mom is here." My tone is grim.

Royal mumbles a curse. "That's not your mom, Loveday. She's dead. I promise you."

Before this mission, I would have believed him without question. But that was before I found out he'd been lying to me about Clarity's paternity. Before I found out that he cheated on my mom with a Sicilian woman who happened to be the daughter of a mobster. Before.

Arnoni gets in the gleaming ebony vehicle and slams the door in my mom's face. The car rolls slowly out of the parking lot, leaving her standing alone.

"I have to talk to her."

"Stay in the van." Royal's voice is tight.

"No." I push past Darnay and fling open the van door, jumping down and sprinting across the parking lot at top speed. Legs pumping, heart pounding, I reach up and take out my earbud, turning it off and dropping it into my bra. Whatever my mom says, it's not something everyone needs to hear. This moment is for us alone.

I'm there in seconds, and my mother is turning toward the sound of running feet, face pale. But when she sees me, a bright smile breaks across her features.

Out of the corner of my eye, the hangar door opens and Royal bursts out. He freezes, eyebrows raised, at the sight of me standing mere feet away from my mom.

Starling and Lotus come running around the corner of the

large, metal building, halting just behind Royal.

At my back, Clarity and Darnay step down out of the van. The skin on the back of my neck pricks as if I can feel their eyes on me. Everyone on my team is focused on my mom and me.

And then, she says something only three people in the world know—my real name.

# Chapter 27

Questions whirl in my head, but at the same time a wave of relief wells up in me. After more than sixteen years, I'm within earshot of both my parents.

"Everyone inside," Royal says, voice low. "We have to get out of sight." He's trying to protect us from the eyes of anyone who happens to be passing by, or flying over, the airfield.

I can't take my eyes off my mom. She takes me hand, and my skin warms at the sensation of having her fingers wrapped around mine. Her snug grip signals that she doesn't want to let go. And I don't want her to, not ever.

I follow my mom's gaze; if looks could kill, Royal would be a goner.

What had Royal said when I asked him about the night she died? Or, more accurately, the night we thought she died?

*"Your mom and I had a pretty nasty fight."*

A thought burns white hot in my brain. What if my mom found out about Clarity, and that's what my parents were fighting about that night? What if she found out about Royal's extramarital activities, packed up her most precious baby girl, and left?

I don't even have to ask him to know in my core that it's

the truth. He's been hiding it from me for all these years, and I know why. He guessed, correctly, that if I ever found out the circumstances surrounding my mom's death, I'd never forgive him for it. And he's exactly right.

Except that now, looking at my mom, there isn't any room in me for anger. I'm bursting with relief that she's alive and standing right beside me.

Clarity sidles up and takes my free hand. "Hi," she says, giving the woman to my right a tentative smile.

My mom's eyes light at the sight of her. "You must be Antonia. I've been wanting to meet you for a long time."

Clarity bites her lip, her face glowing. "I go by Clarity, actually, but I've been wanting to meet you too." Impulsively, my sister crosses and throws her arms around the woman, squeezing her tight. She returns the gesture with one hand, patting my sister's back.

Once Clarity pulls away, my mom slides her right hand into the pocket of her knee-length sweater-jacket.

I tug my hand down to bring her focus back to me. "If you wanted to see us," I whisper, "how come you've stayed away for the past sixteen years?" I try to keep any tinge of frustration out of my voice, and mostly succeed.

My mom looks away, casting her face down to the floor. "Your dad didn't let me see you."

"What?" I gasp. "That can't be. There's no way he'd keep us apart."

She shrugs. "I don't know what to else to say."

Royal steps toward us, and my mom sneers at him, tightening her grip on my hand.

When he draws close, she bristles. "You won't separate us again. I won't let you."

My dad's eyes narrow as he watches her, studying her face,

her hair, and the way she's holding herself. He turns his focus to me. "Loveday, this woman is not your mother."

"How can you say that?" I burst out, gesturing toward her with both hands. "Look at her."

"Please, step outside and talk to me."

I'm about to glare at him and tell him where to go, but his expression brings me up short. He's actually pleading, silently, with me, and I have never seen him do that before.

I loosen my hold on my mom's hand, but she refuses to let go. "Don't go with him," she says, angry. "He'll never let me see you again."

My eyes lock on hers. "I won't let that happen. I'll be right back."

Her mouth falls into an open frown and her shoulders sag, but my mom releases my hand.

Royal brushes past her toward the side door, and I follow. "Lotus," he says over his shoulder. "Plug this into your computer and test it on yourself. See what it comes up with." He hands over the external drive to Lotus's eager hands, then swings open the door. Once he's through, my dad turns to make sure I'm following him.

I take one more long look at my mom before crossing the room and following Royal outside.

He's standing with his back against the corrugated metal structure, hands resting in the pockets of his slacks. His mouth opens, but I hold up a hand.

"Before you say anything, I have to know. Were you fighting about Clarity the night of the car accident? Is that why she packed me up and left?"

Royal hangs his head. "She found some emails from Clarity's mom, Giada—"

"I know their names."

At the look of surprise on his face, I continue. "Clarity found an article about a couple that died during the earthquake, and the dates matched up. She figured it was her biological parents."

He nods. "She's right. Her mother was Giada Arnoni, and her father—"

"Is you."

Another slow nod.

"How long?" I ask, my voice grinding out between my clenched teeth.

"What?"

"How long were you cheating on my mom with Mrs. Arnoni?" I emphasize each word, making my disgust at his actions plain.

"It was one weekend. Your mom and I were struggling. We hadn't been connecting for a while, and then the CIA sent me to Sicily to look into la nostra società. I met Giada, and she was lonely. Her husband was always off working for her father. You've met him. Beppe Arnoni. And we, we…" His voice trailed off.

"I get the gist," I say, my words clipped.

"So nine months later, I got an email from Giada, telling me that she'd had a baby girl, and she was positive she was mine. She sent me a photo." Royal lifts his watch to his face and scrolls for a minute before holding his arm out so I can see the screen. On it there's a photo of a beautiful, tan, toddler girl with wavy brunette hair and large brown eyes.

"Antonia." It's a struggle to tear my eyes away from the sweet, tiny baby on the screen, but I manage it. "Back to the night of the accident."

"Your mom stumbled across an email to me from Giada, containing several photos of baby Antonia. She was a smart woman, and she put two and two together. She asked me about it, and I couldn't lie to her, so she packed you up and left. She was fuming, and the streets were slick from a rainstorm. I tried to stop her, but she wouldn't listen to me."

I turn my face away. "I don't want to hear anymore."

Royal's voice breaks. "I'm so sorry. It's all my fault. If I hadn't done it, she might still be with us."

"She's inside," I deadpan.

He shakes his head. "That is not your mother. I'd know her anywhere. Her body language, her voice, it's wrong. I don't know who—" He stops, his head inclining to one side, his gaze moving past me across the parking lot. "Unless." He spins and goes inside, moving briskly, not even stopping to hold the door for me, which he usually does.

I run behind him. "What's going on?" I call after him, but he doesn't answer.

Inside, Lotus is off in one corner working at his laptop, with Julep, Starling, and Darnay hovering over his shoulders. They glance up at the sound of our entrance, but then their focus returns to the computer. Lotus is typing quickly, his brow furrowed.

Royal strides across the space to where my mom is standing, and he stops abruptly in front of her, frowning.

Clarity steps toward me. "Are you okay?" she whispers in my ear.

"No," I respond. "But I will be, eventually."

She gives me a light kiss on the cheek. "I left my jacket in the van. I'll be right back." She leaves the hangar without making a sound.

"Roll up your right pant leg," Royal commands my mom.

Her eyes widen. "What? No." Her voice is high, barely controlled.

203

"Do it, or I will do it for you." He kneels in front of her, hands at the ready.

The woman looks to me for help.

I step forward. "Dad? Why do you want her to roll up her pants?"

He sighs and turns to me. "Your mom had a scar on her calf from where she knocked over a floor fan and cut herself." A smile plays on his lips. "She was rather clumsy, your mom."

I finish his train of thought, locking eyes with the woman I'm almost completely positive is my mom. "If you're really my mom, you'll have a scar. It'll be proof."

"Guys," Lotus interrupts.

"What?" Royal and I ask at the same time.

"We've got a problem."

# Chapter 28

Royal's shoulders droop. "Another one?"

Lotus nods. "It's a big one. Come look at this."

My dad marches across the hangar to where the rest of the team is standing around Lotus's laptop. "What is it?" Royal asks.

"I'm pretty sure the demonstration The Chin gave you was faked. The facial recognition software hack isn't on this drive." Lotus's face is lined with worry.

"What do you mean?" Royal asks.

"I mean, it doesn't give me access to the CIA facial recognition databases, or anything, really. He sold you a worthless external hard drive."

Royal clenches his jaw. "He must still have it squirreled away somewhere."

"At least we know where he is," Starling says as he walks over to the corner of the room where The Chin and the auctioneer are still out cold. He prods the man's leg with the toe of his shoe, but The Chin doesn't flinch. He's still out cold.

"Wake him up," Royal commands.

"Does anyone have the antidote?" I ask as I move toward the two slumbering men. Usually I carry a vial or two of it in my utility belt, but in my haste to leave the Tower, I forgot to pack some. And even if I had packed it, all my gear is across the parking lot in the van.

"Right here." Starling holds up a small vial of clear liquid. He meets me in the corner and hands it over.

"Needle?" I ask.

"Um." He opens one of the pockets in his cargo pants and pulls out a sterile needle still in its packaging.

"Thanks."

My fingers close around it and I rip it open. After unscrewing the cap of the vial, I pull the plunger to suck up some of the liquid into the needle. Gauging the amount of antidote needed is not an exact science, so I eyeball the measuring lines on the side of the plastic chamber until I've got what I calculate is the right amount, based on a quick mental estimate of The Chin's body weight. Then I kneel beside the black market seller, shove his sleeve up his arm, and locate the vein in the crook of his elbow. In a smooth motion, I insert the needle into his vein. Fortunately, my victim has large, pulsing veins, so I get it on the first try. A slow depression of the plunger pushes the antidote into the vein, and relief rises in me. Sticking people with a needle is not my favorite part of my job.

"Wow," Starling says. "If spying doesn't work out for you, you'd be an awesome phlebotomist."

"Thanks." I let out a titter. "But I'm planning on being a spy forever."

It takes a couple minutes, but The Chin's eyes snap open and he lunges toward me, arms outstretched. A cry escapes him, but Darnay thrusts his leg out, knocking the man backward.

"What's going on?" The Chin yells. "What did you do to me? Help! Somebody!" His voice increases in volume until he's shouting the last bit.

Lotus calls from where he and Julep are sitting behind the laptop. "No one can hear you."

The Chin opens his mouth to yell again, but Royal pulls his firearm from the holster at his waist and levels it in the man's face. "Where is the software hack?" Royal's voice is low but firm.

The Chin's eyes widen, but then he puts on a smarmy look and simpers at him, despite having a gun in his face. "Whatever do you mean? You have the hack on the drive I just gave you. I demonstrated it for you, remember?"

"You and I both know it was fake. Now tell me where it really is." Royal's eyes narrow at the man, who leans back, drawing away from the gun Darnay is pointing at him.

The Chin looks to each of us in turn, his eyes landing on Darnay, who is standing behind Royal with his hands clasped in front of him, but receives no help.

"Tell us," Darnay says, his voice gruff.

The Chin sighs and turns his attention back to Royal. "It's gone. I already sold it."

"You what?" I explode, stepping toward him, fists clenched.

The Chin shrieks. "Keep her away from me!"

"Loveday," Royal says quietly.

I meet his eyes and step back, but I keep on giving the scummy guy my best scowl.

"You sold it already," Darnay says, "to who?"

The man's eyes shift between Darnay and Royal, as if he's not sure who he should tell.

"Well?" Darnay prods.

After a moment, The Chin seems to decide to address the man with the gun, because he pushes up to his knees in front of my dad. "Here's the thing," he starts, rubbing his hands together as if he's putting on hand lotion. "I was hired to steal it, and right after I did the job, I gave it to the individual who contracted me to do it."

"Then why did you hold the auction?" I ask. "Didn't you worry about pissing off whoever tried to buy it from you?" I lift my arm to sweep over the room. "There were some pretty powerful people here today."

He shrugs. "I needed the money."

I roll my eyes.

Royal cuts to the chase. "Who paid you to steal the software hack?"

"I, I don't know his, or her, real name." He holds his hands up in supplication toward me, as if acknowledging that the possibility that the criminal might be a woman would mollify me. It doesn't.

He continues. "All I know is…" He stands. "Look, I'll tell you, but I have the distinct feeling that this person will kill me if they find out I squealed, so you've gotta help me."

"Don't worry; where you're going, no one will be able to get to you."

The Chin sags at this, licking his lips. "I know a codename."

"What is it?" I ask.

"Nexus." It's a whisper, so quiet I'm not quite sure what I heard. I turn the name over in my brain, trying to remember if I've ever heard it before. But the rigid way my dad is standing tells me he's heard it before, and the frown on his face says it's not a good thing.

"Royal, what is it?" I move toward him as he lowers his gun and returns it to its holster.

Royal's eyes flit to Darnay. "Charles, keep an eye on him,

will you?"

Darnay gives him a nod, and Royal stalks off to the other side of the room, near where Lotus is sitting. I notice that Lotus's arm is slung over the back of Julep's chair, but she's sitting forward, back straight, so they're not touching at all.

Royal stops and turns to face me, his eyes focused on the corner where Darnay is standing over The Chin and the still-prostrate form of the auctioneer.

I put a hand on his arm to draw his attention back to me. "Who is Nexus?" I ask, tugging at the fabric of his jacket sleeve.

"I haven't heard that name in almost twenty years," he says, a slight tremor in his voice.

It's this chink in his control that gets my hackles up. "Who is he?" I ask again.

Royal swallows. "About eighteen years ago, there were several suspicious agent deaths. Freak accidents during what should have been easy jobs. One man was smashed by a rising elevator, for example."

My blood chills at this. "That's pretty gruesome."

Royal gives a nod. "It was. We thought… That is, The CIA thought it was someone inside who'd gone bad, but they never found any proof, and after a few months, Nexus disappeared."

"I wonder why he was killing agents. Do you think he turned traitor?"

Royal's eyes drag across the hangar to where The Chin is standing, shuffling on his feet. "No. The deaths, they always felt personal to me, like someone trying to get revenge, but for what?"

"So why would he resurface now, after all these years?"

"I don't know."

My eyes follow his over the hangar. Darnay is standing in front of The Chin, blocking him from moving out of the corner. Starling is a few feet behind Darnay, watching all three of the men in the corner. Julep and Lotus are still working at the computer, but the frustrated looks on their faces hint that they aren't making any progress. My mom is sitting in a chair near the now-empty table the catering company had used to serve snacks during the auction.

"Clarity," I whisper. "She's been gone a while."

"What?" Royal turns to me, a question in his eyes.

"She went to the van to get her sweater." I glance down at my watch. "How long has she been gone?"

A laugh rings out, echoing off the walls of the giant metal box we're in. It cuts through me like an icy wind on a freezing day in DC.

My mother—she's laughing as she rises from her chair. "Your sister isn't here anymore." The sturdy way she says it burrows down to my core, making my heart beat frantically.

In a second I'm out the door, plummeting across the parking lot to the van. The sliding door hangs open, but there's no one inside. I jump inside and make for the front seat where Clarity had stowed her things. Her sweater is right there, laying across the seat.

I'm out of the van and scanning the parking lot. It's empty of cars and she's nowhere to be seen. I pump my legs, pushing myself to run as fast as I can down the road away from the hangar, across the tarmac. A taxiing plane glides toward me and I jump out of the way, fighting to keep my breathing even.

The plane takes flight and I spin to watch it rise into the air. My sister could be on that plane.

There are several other planes on the runway, waiting for their turn to take off. She could be on any one of these planes.

But my heart drops. I know she's not on any of these planes. She's only been gone a handful of minutes, but in my gut I know she's out of my reach. A primal scream escapes me as I whip around and run back to the hangar, where my teammates are standing outside the door.

"Loveday! Clarity!" Lotus's cries reach me as I move within earshot.

"She's not here," I yell back, willing my tears to remain behind my eyes. I burst into the hangar and leap toward my mom, shoving her to the ground. "Why were you talking to Beppe Arnoni?" I yell, leaning down into her face. My hand reaches down to grab my gun, but my fingers close on air. I realize with a jolt that I'm not wearing my holster. "How do you know him? Where is my sister?"

Royal's hand is on mine, gently removing it from the leather strap that holds my handgun in place.

My mom gives him a wicked smile as she puts her hand in her sweater and pulls out a tiny electronic device about the size of a ladybug, with a tiny raised button on one side. It's a Bennington 6—one of the best tracking devices on the market. A neon green light emanates from the device, making it clear that it's on and functioning as it's designed to do.

I scramble toward her, intent on using my fists to pound the information out of her, but Starling is at my side, putting an arm around my waist, hauling me backward.

"Let me go!" I yell, pushing against him. I'm strong, but he's stronger. His grip holds.

"Loveday," he whispers in my ear.

I stop fighting, and go still, my back pressed against his solid form. Instead of feeling awkward, like I thought it would, it's reassuring having him, this constant, at my back.

Starling cautiously lowers his arm, his eyes asking me if I'm okay, or if I'm going to go ape-wild on the woman again.

I turn my cold eyes to her, but I don't move.

Her gaze flickers to me before settling on Royal. "It's all your fault," she sneers. "You have only yourself to blame."

When he doesn't stop her, she continues. "You killed my sister, so I've taken your daughter from you. You'll never see her again. The Arnonis will see to that."

"No!" I scream, lunging for her again. One fist lands in her face before both Starling and Lotus are pulling me back, dragging me away from her. Where minutes ago my heart was bursting with hope, now there is only hatred. She's my aunt, not my mother. Instead of repairing the hole in my family, she has dug her fingers into it, rending it into jagged pieces.

"You're her sister," Royal says, his voice beginning to crack.

She nods, chin high. "Forgot about me, didn't you? But I didn't forget."

"I never forgot," he says, "But it's hard to keep up with family in my line of work. You were safer not knowing…"

"She wasn't safer!" The woman spits. "She knew, and it killed her. You killed her."

"Why help the Arnonis take my daughter? She's innocent of all this."

"I was teaching in Sicily, and I got on Beppe's wrong side. He's rather touchy about his grandchildren."

My eyebrows raise. That's true.

"He told me he'd forget about my poor treatment of his grandson, if I'd do him a favor. He knew I was from New Jersey, you see, and he asked me to go back to the East coast to do a little poking around for him. He said one of his granddaughters was there, and he wanted me to find her.

Imagine my surprise when not only do I find Antonia Arnoni, I find that the family she's staying with is my very own niece and brother-in-law. So I decided to have a little fun."

Recognition hits me. She's been wandering around DC looking for Clarity. That's why I've seen her in odd places. "You've been trolling me for months." I throw the words at her, anger seeping out of my skin.

"That's right," she says. "Fun, eh? Thinking you're seeing the dead ghost of your mother."

I pale at this. "You're pure evil."

"The thirst for revenge will do that to you," she says, eyeing me. "I'd be careful if I were you. You could turn into me."

"Never."

Royal turns to me. "You've seen this woman before, and you never told me?" His question is quiet, but I can hear the hurt in his voice.

"How would you react if I told you I had seen my dead mom? You'd think I was losing my mental faculties. You'd pull me out of the field. Oh, wait…" I trail off, glaring at him.

"So, where's Clarity?" Lotus puts in. "We want her back."

Her eyes are deadly cold as she locks on Royal. "Can you feel it? The jittery panic as the realization hits you that you might never see the person you love again? I know exactly what it's like." She licks her lips. "You can scour the earth, but you'll never get her back. Just like I'll never get my sister back. And now we're even."

I roll my shoulders, my stance square, my emotions barely in check. "You say that now, but you just took a blowtorch to a bridge you can never rebuild. And we will get Clarity back, because we're the best damn teenage spies in the world. And what are you? Nothing." I spin away from her, motioning to my teammates as I move across the hangar. "Royal?" I ask. "Do you have any objections to a detour through Sicily?"

"None," he responds.

"Then get your gear, team. We have a plane to catch."

# About the Author

Emily lives in sunny Southern California with her husband and daughters. She started writing in elementary school and continued writing in college, where she earned a degree in creative writing. She often gets ideas for stories from the lives of her friends and family. When she's not writing, she enjoys cuddling with her two dachshunds Nestlé and Kiefer, crocheting, watching television, and enjoying the sunshine with her daughters and their flock of backyard chickens.

To learn more about Emily, visit her website: www.emilykazmierski.com

Keep reading for a sneak peek at book three of the Ivory Tower Spies series, *Spy Your Heart Out.*

# Chapter 1

Confusion crackles around the airplane hangar.

"What plane?" Royal asks, catching my arm before I can bolt out of the building.

I shake off his hand. "My private plane. How else do you think I got here? All of the commercial airlines are booked for the Olympics."

He levies a stern look at me. "How did you pay for a private plane?"

"About that. I may have compromised one of the entrances to our hideout. And Summer knows I'm not an ordinary teenager."

"Summer," Royal says, the lines on his face deepening.

"Summer, as in your boss at the concierge desk?" Lotus asks.

When I raise my eyebrows to indicate that he's correct, his hand flies up to cup his mouth. "Oh, you're in it now."

Beside Lotus, Julep's eyes are wide as she watches the exchange.

I shrug quickly. I was already in enough trouble, and I haven't had time to think about how mad Royal will be once he hears the next bit. I eye him, and he gestures with one hand for me to continue.

"She saw me coming out of the waterfall." I shake my head, pushing away that line of thought. "But that's not important. All that matters is that we get Clarity back. Beppe Arnoni took her and I bet they're going straight back to his lair in Palermo, wherever it is."

Royal's jaw clenches. "We'll talk about Summer later. Right now, we need to confirm that Clarity isn't in the area around the airport." He lifts his watch and pushes several of its buttons with his free hand. "I've pinged her watch. It looks like it's near the entrance to the airport. Julep can you…"

But I'm off at a run before he can finish his statement. My legs pump with all their might as I careen down the taxiway toward the entrance gate to the airport. Several airport employees wave at me, yelling in Russian, but I ignore them. One of them, a tall, lanky guy with a shaved head and a goatee, gives chase, but I outstrip him easily. Being twenty years younger and in excellent shape gives me the advantage.

Running at a full-out sprint, I pass the terminal on my left. I'm only a few hundred yards from the airport entrance now, and begin to slow. "Send me the location of Clarity's watch," I huff into my earbud between long, controlled breaths.

My watch pings and I look down at its screen. According to this, Clarity is only about fifty yards ahead of me. I scan the area, but all I can see is the road into and out of the airport, lined by empty, brown fields on both sides. I slip past the gate and stop. The map on my watch screen shows that I'm right on top of Clarity, but she's not here. There isn't anyone out here.

Across the road, there's a large building complex that looks like a shopping center. "How accurate are the locators on our watches?" I ask.

"Down to the foot," Royal responds.

I curse under my breath. "She's not here." I pivot slowly in a full circle. "She's not here."

"Look around you. See if you can find her watch."

Even though I know he can't see me right now, I bob my head. My eyes study the ground around as I turn in another circle, steps careful and measured. A shrub by the road catches my attention. I cross the pavement toward it and kneel down. The tiny, dry branches scratch at my arms as I push them aside to peer at the dirt below the plant. Clarity's watch is there, and its face is cracked, but still working. "I found it. He must have tossed it out his car window."

Tears come unbidden to the backs of my eyes, and I lean back into a low squat, swiping at my cheeks with my empty left hand. Clarity's watch is clutched in my right. A sniff escapes me.

A voice comes through my earbud. "Loveday, are you all right?" It's the first thing Starling has said in several minutes.

"Fine," I grind out, before pushing to a stand and walking back toward the airplane hangar at the far side of the airport.

This time, the airport personnel on the ground don't pay any attention to me. They're busy flagging a plane down the runway. At the sight of it, I freeze. It's a mid-sized passenger plane with the logo of a top European airline emblazoned on the side. "Dad!" I yell. "We have to ground the planes. Clarity could be on one of them."

"I don't have that kind of power."

"We don't have time to argue." I'm running again, but this time I'm heading straight for the passenger plane. If I can beat it to the runway, they'll have to stop. My leg muscles push hard, harder than ever before, but still the plane is going to get there first.

"Help me!" I yell.

"Loveday, stop," Royal responds. "You're not faster than a commercial airplane."

Without looking, I know that he's standing outside the hangar, watching me.

"I have to try." But my legs are already slowing. Royal is right; I'm no match for a craft that size. It pulls ahead of me down the runway, picking up speed as it advances.

Clarity might be on that plane, but there's nothing I can do in this moment to stop it from taking off.

The plane's frontal landing gear leaves the ground. Its nose tips upward. The aircraft's back end follows, and it's as good as gone.

I stand, transfixed, watching as the vessel disappears into the white sky.

"Hey."

That one little word makes me jump. But it's not Clarity standing there when I turn to look.

It's Starling.

His face is trained on me, and his eyes shutter back and forth across my face, gauging my expression.

My face falls in a frown. "I lost her." Sadness rises in me, filling me up until I'm sure it will slosh out if I don't stand completely still.

Starling gives a slight shake of his head. "You didn't lose her. She was stolen from you. None of this is your fault."

"That's not what it feels like," I say, and again the tears threaten to spill over. I don't let them. My teeth bite down on my tongue, and slowly the unwanted waterworks recede.

"Let's go back," the tall boy standing at my side says, gesturing toward the hangar with his thumb.

I take a deep breath, and nod.

Starling slings one arm over my shoulder, and pats my upper arm with tentative fingers.

It's a surprise even to me that I don't want to shove him off and get as far away as possible. Instead, Starling's touch has a steadying effect on me as we walk side by side back to the hangar. I fall into step with him, taking two steps for every one of his, since he's so much taller than I am.

When I don't push him away, Starling smiles. "You run amazingly fast in heels."

My lips curve in a faint smile, but I don't look directly at him. I'm too busy watching Royal stare at us from across the apron. "I've had lots of practice."

He lowers his head toward mine, speaking in a low voice. "It shows."

If I wasn't trained to hide my emotions, I might have blushed at that comment.

Once we reach the hangar, Royal steps aside for Starling to go inside, but when I move to follow, he blocks my path.

Our eyes meet, and my face falls. I'm in trouble. Again.

He steps around the corner of the building, waiting for me to follow him.

I'm barely there when he speaks.

"You can't run off like that again. It's not safe."

"I had to see if Clarity was still here—"

"No. You wait for orders, or I'll send you straight home and go on to Sicily without you."

I glare at him. "You wouldn't."

His chin lifts. "Try me. This is exactly why I took you off the team in the first place." He doesn't flinch at my scowl, so we're locked in a staring contest for several seconds. The silence around us deepens, but still neither of us moves to break the stalemate.

A groan sounds over Royal's right shoulder.

It's the security guard The Chin hired, waking up from being tranqed.

Royal pulls his tranquilizer gun from his belt, twists at the waist, and fires another dart into the barely conscious man's thigh. The man's head falls back into the long grass, and a snore emits from his nose. He's out again.

When Royal looks back at me, I open my mouth and push out the words. "I won't run off."

"Promise me."

Fighting an eye roll, I say, "I promise."

"Good. Now let's get back inside."

We step into the hangar, and Royal locks the door behind us. "The first step," he calls to Lotus and Julep, who are huddled around the table where his laptop sits, "is to confirm that it was Beppe Arnoni who took Clarity." He strides across the building and sits in the chair recently vacated by Lotus. "Hopefully we've got a satellite in the area that I can access. See if we can find images of Clarity outside in the last half hour."

My eyebrows rise at this. It's going to take forever to do that, when we already know exactly what happened. Knowing I'm on thin ice, I speak in a slow, controlled tone. "Don't you think that will take too long?" When he doesn't respond, I try a different tactic. "Clarity must be scared, wondering if we've noticed she's missing."

This time Royal looks up at me. "Stop pushing," my dad says, voice even, as he types on his keyboard. "I know you're positive he took Clarity, but we have to make sure first. It won't do us any good to fly to Sicily only to discover that Mr. Arnoni isn't there." Casting a cold look at my aunt, he sets to work typing.

"This is going to take forever," I mutter, sinking into the nearest folding chair. All the exertion of the last few minutes, coupled with the lack of sleep, is taking its toll. I fold my arms, placing my hands behind my head, and lean back in the chair. Yet, my mind won't slow down. My thoughts are spiraling further into the black unknown, and with each minute that passes it feels like Clarity is slipping farther away.

# Chapter 2

Starling eases across the floor and takes up a position against the wall, mere feet away from me. I can feel his eyes on my back, but I don't turn to meet them.

Julep crosses the hangar and stands, looking down at me. "We'll get her back," she whispers.

My gaze rises to her face, and she reaches out to give my shoulder a squeeze.

"Thanks."

"Starling," Royal says, looking at us over the top of his laptop.

"Yes, sir?" he asks, a few feet from my chair.

"Go into the airport terminal, and see if Arnoni and Clarity are inside. There's a possibility that he's attempting to take a flight from here."

"Yes, sir." He stands upright and makes for the door, closing it gently behind him.

I bolt out of my chair, but Royal stops me with a slow shake of his head. "You stay here."

I frown, plopping back down in my chair. My arms cross tightly over my chest, and my eyes fall to my matte black heels. They're sturdy leather with tiny bows over the toes. Even though they're more overtly feminine than the clothes and shoes I usually wear, I like them. They didn't kill my feet when I ran across the airport, which is a hard quality to find in high heels.

"There it is!" Royal says with enthusiasm in his voice.

My interest perks at this, pushing me upward in my chair.

"Lotus," Royal calls. "Come look through this footage for any traces of Arnoni returning to the parking lot outside, or of Clarity leaving."

"Will do."

Royal stands, and Lotus takes his seat at the laptop. My dad pulls his phone from his pocket and makes a call. "Haru?" He is silent as Haru talks on the other end of the line, his mouth forming an amused smile.

It almost makes me laugh. She's probably prattling on about something she's excited about, not realizing that there's a reason for his call other than to check in on her.

"That's great," Royal says, "but let me stop you there. We've got a problem here, and I need your help. Use the security codes I gave you to access the airport's departure schedule. Find all of the flights leaving here today and tomorrow that land in Italy, France, Austria, Switzerland, Slovenia, or Croatia. Scan their passenger lists for Beppe Arnoni and Antonia Arnoni." He falls silent again. "I understand. Get back to me when you can." He hangs up and deposits the phone in the pocket of his slacks. Then, he makes for the door. "I'll be right back."

"Where are you going?" I ask, leaning forward in my chair.

"To call my contact at the CIA. They'll have to send someone to pick up our friend, over there." He nods toward where The Chin is sulking in the corner, still handcuffed to a table leg.

"But who knows how long that will take. We have to be ready to go the minute we've confirmed Arnoni kidnapped Clarity."

Royal sighs and walks back over to where I'm standing. Lowering his voice, he speaks. "I'm in a hurry to get her back too, but we were hired to do a job, and we have to finish it. We have to deliver The Chin into the custody of a U.S. government official before we can leave St. Petersburg."

My shoulders slump. He's right. We have to finish our job. It will put Arnoni a few hours ahead of us, but I don't think he'll hurt Clarity. She's his granddaughter, a member of his family, biologically, at least. And from the way he spoke about his grandson when I saw him in Palermo, family means something to him. Something important.

"What are we going to do with the traitor?"

Royal's eyebrows rise in question.

"My so-called aunt?"

"The embassy agent will take her into custody as well."

I purse my lips.

"What?"

"I was hoping we'd leave her here to rot in a Russian prison. I bet the conditions aren't as nice here as in our prisons back home."

He rolls his eyes at me. "We aren't leaving her here to rot. We'll have her taken back to the U.S. to be charged and tried. It's the just thing to do."

"What's with you and upholding the letter of the law?"

Royal smirks. It's a look I haven't seen on his face in, maybe, ever. "I wasn't always such an upstanding citizen."

I nudge him with my elbow. "Are you sure about that? You seem pretty squeaky clean to me." I flash a smile.

"I will have you know, Charles and I broke lots of rules, back in our day."

"What, like jaywalking?"

The man chuckles. "I'll be right back."

225

I watch him go. At least now I know where I get the sarcastic streak from. I always guessed my mom had been the snarky one, but maybe I was wrong.

The door swings open again, and I turn to look. "That was quick…" I say, before I see that it's Starling entering the room, not Royal.

"Anything?" I ask.

A frown on his face, Starling meets my eyes and gives a shake of his head.

Impatient, I start chewing on the inside of my lip.

Next to The Chin, the auctioneer begins to stir. A low groan escapes him as he pushes himself off the floor with both hands, rising to a seated position. His eyes widen at the sight of The Chin handcuffed next to him. "What's going on?" he says, his voice higher than it was during the auction, laced with a note of panic. He tries to scramble to his feet, but I block his path before he can take a step.

"You're going to have to stay here with us for a few minutes," I say, not moving my eyes from him.

"Why?" He glances over my shoulder. "Oh." His eyes widen and he takes several steps back into the corner of the hangar, hands raised.

Julep comes up beside me, brandishing her tranquilizer gun. "Do as she says."

He nods vigorously. "I will."

I handcuff him to the leg on the opposite end of the table from The Chin, and leave him there, trembling and grumbling under his breath.

The hangar door squeaks as it swings open, and Royal steps inside. "Any luck yet?" he calls to Lotus, who merely shakes his head, his gaze fixed on the computer screen.

Royal nods, his expression grim, before turning to me. "The embassy is sending someone to extradite The Chin, and your aunt, back to the U.S., and we're to wait here until the agent arrives."

My lips flatten into a tight line, but I say nothing. Even though I understand why we're waiting around, it still feels like we're twiddling our thumbs, when everyone in this building knows Arnoni's taken Clarity back to Sicily. But I don't belabor the point. Instead, I cross the hangar, flip a chair around, and plop down onto it backward so I'm a few feet in front of my aunt.

She's handcuffed to the chair now, but there's an easy expression on her face. Her eyes float up to mine, and there's a glimmer of what might be interest, but then it fades.

I watch her for a beat, waiting to see if she'll say anything. Finally, she does.

"You look a lot like her, you know."

I tilt my head to one side in response.

"Does he tell you that a lot?" she asks, the hint of a smile on her lips. "That you have her features?"

"Are we really going to sit here and talk about my mother, instead of talking about how you just betrayed your family for a mob boss?"

Her eyebrows rise at this, and she leans back in her chair, away from me. The handcuff on her wrist keeps her from crossing both arms over her chest, so she settles for one, her fingers cupped around her opposite elbow. "He deserves this." Her tone is harsh and flat.

"But I don't, and neither does Clarity. Is revenge more important to you than the fates of your nieces?"

This makes her wince, but she doesn't respond. Instead, she casts her glance over toward Royal, who is standing at Lotus's back, helping comb through the images on the laptop screen. Her hackles rise as she watches him. It's as if merely looking at him fills her with revulsion. When she looks back toward me, she's practically snarling. "I won't apologize," she says.

"I didn't ask you to," I say, pushing out of my chair. It's clear I'm not going to get anywhere talking to her right now, so I join the boys crowded around the laptop.

Lotus points at the screen, freezing the image there. "There! There she is."

Sure enough, Clarity's in the photo, walking casually toward the surveillance van, her hand over her eyes to block the sunlight.

"Finally," Royal says. The sag of his shoulders hints at the relief he's feeling at finally spotting Clarity in the satellite footage.

My sister must have left her sunglasses somewhere… I cast around the hangar, and there they are, abandoned on one of the folding chairs. I jog over to retrieve them, placing the oversized frames on the top of my head before returning to where my team is huddled at the table.

"Okay, so from there, she walks over to the van…" Lotus is narrating the footage as it unspools before our eyes.

"There's his car," I say as my eyes catch the vehicle pulling back into the lot. "The plates are the same."

In the video, Clarity halts in place, watching as the car pulls to a stop and Arnoni steps out.

All we can see is her back, but it's obvious the moment she realizes who it is: her entire body tenses, but she doesn't move. Instead, she watches to see what he's going to do.

Arnoni takes a step toward her, his mouth moving in smooth words. We can't hear him, of course, but I can't help but strain to make out the words. It's too bad I'm not a great lip reader. I make a mental note to work on it once we get my sister back.

As Arnoni takes another step toward Clarity, she shakes her head.

He advances another step, and my sister turns to run back toward the hanger, her eyes wide.

That's when he pulls the tazer out of his jacket pocket.

Clarity's entire body goes stiff, and she hits the ground, immobilized.

"Oooh," Lotus groans, furrowing his eyebrows.

"That little… I'll, I'll…" I can't form words for how angry I am. No, I can. I want to murder that bastard, slowly, so he can feel his lifeblood leaving his body. But I can't verbalize that. I'm pretty sure Royal would send me on the first flight back to D.C. if he heard me talking like that. He's not a fan of unnecessary bloodshed, and I bet he'd disagree with me about whether killing Beppe Arnoni is exactly necessary.

I manage to keep my mouth shut, but he must sense what I'm thinking because he puts one hand on my shoulder, pressing gently until I turn to meet his eyes. "We'll make sure he pays a just price for hurting her. Trust me."

All I can muster is a curt nod, which he accepts. "Lotus, send this over to the embassy with a write up so they know what they're looking at. And make it short."

"Yes, sir," Lotus says, leaning forward over the keyboard and typing quickly.

"Starling, go back into the terminal and get everyone some food. I'm sure we all could use it."

"I will." Starling's eyes meet mine for a second before he turns to go. Without saying anything, he's asking me if I'm okay.

My eyes scream back: No. No. No!

He stands still for a second, but then he leaves. He has orders, after all.

I let my head fall backward as I stand awkwardly behind Lotus, watching him type.

Royal's phone rings and he answers. "Haru."

I close my eyes, hoping that she's found Arnoni's travel plans and that he hasn't left the area yet. If he's still here, it shouldn't be difficult to get Clarity back. He won't have all of the resources he will have if he makes it back to Palermo.

But Royal's face doesn't lighten as he listens, and I already know what he's going to say even before he hangs up.

"She's already gone." The words are sure, even as they leave my mouth.

"The plane left half an hour ago, mere minutes after he grabbed her."

"Ugh!" I stomp one foot on the ground, wishing I had my trench coat on so I could shove my clenched fists into its deep pockets.

The hangar door bangs open.

"What now?" I spin toward the door to see The Chin's bodyguard standing there, taking in the scene. His suit's rumpled and he has a bit of grass on one shoulder, but his small, stone-like eyes are bright and aware.

"What's going on in here?" he asks, voice gruff through his Russian accent.

"Igor!" The Chin yells. "Get me out of here."

"It's EYE-gor," the man responds, the frustration clear in his voice. They've obviously had this conversation before.

"Same difference!"

Igor huffs and scans the room, his eyes moving over Lotus, Julep, Royal, and me, who are standing facing him, guns drawn. All except me. My stupid guns are still in the van.

"How much is he paying you?" Royal asks, his eyes not moving from the bodyguard's features.

"Not enough." And with that, Igor exits the hangar, leaving The Chin spluttering in the corner.

"Guess you're stuck with us," Lotus says.

I titter. It feels good to release some of the tension building up in me. I'm a woman of action. I'm not used to having to wait on another person to complete a mission. This state of suspension is going to be the death of me.

Preorder *Spy Your Heart Out*, book three of the Ivory Tower Spies series on Amazon.com.